～ *Romantic Times Library* ～

Outside the flashes of lightning were no longer so bright; thunder still rumbled, but from a distance.

S*ighing contentedly, Leah snuggled closer to Jace, closing her eyes, resting her hand on his chest. After their heart rates returned to normal, she stirred only once.*

"I love you," she murmured as she fell asleep.

Silently, Jace brushed her tousled hair back from her temples and placed a lingering kiss on her brow.

Romantic Times Library

Deep in the Heart

Donna Kimel Vitek

BARONET BOOKS
New York, New York

Series Publisher
Anne Waldman Gober

Series Editor
Rochelle Larkin

Copyright © MCMLXXXV
by Donna Kimel Vitek

Published by Playmore Inc., Publishers and
Waldman Publishing Corp.,
New York, NY

All Rights Reserved.

Baronet Books is a trademark of Playmore Inc., Publishers and
Waldman Publishing Corp., New York, New York

No part of this book may be reproduced or copied in any form, or by
any means, electronic, mechanical, photocopying, recording, or
otherwise, without written permission of the publisher.
Printed in Canada

Dear Reader,

Welcome to ROMANTIC TIMES LIBRARY — a collection of romance books that deliver stories of everlasting love, understanding, and commitment.

The book you're holding and the others in the series have been especially selected from <u>Romantic Times</u> Magazine's favorite contemporary novels. The authors include classic American romance writers.

American women deserve to be swept away into worlds of love and ecstasy, and reading romances gives you just that. Many women are even creating a romantic environment for their reading, for what better way to relax with a romance than in a bubble bath with lit candles, or in a cozy nightgown nestled against fluffy pillows!

Please let me know how you enjoy this book and the others in the series, and if you want even more books to choose from in the future.

Think of us as your romance connection. We welcome your letters and will be happy to answer any questions and requests.

Keep romance in your heart and a good book in your hands!

Kathryn Falk, *Lady Barrow*

Romantic Times Magazine
55 Bergen Street
Brooklyn NY 11201
Telephone: (718) 237-1097
E-Mail: RTmag1@aol.com

CHAPTER ONE

Leah Bancroft stared at the woman across the table from her in disbelief. "You must be kidding, Erica," she finally managed to say. "You tell Jace you're leaving him. I'm certainly not going to."

"But—"

"No. And that's final," Leah said emphatically, tucking a wayward tendril of honey-blond hair behind her ear. "I'm not about to get involved in this. Your marital problems are none of my business."

"But it's not a matter of marital problems anymore. It's the end of the marriage," Erica Austin persisted. "And I just hoped you'd do me this one little favor and tell Jace that—"

"Tell him yourself."

"I'd rather not see him. Every time we try to talk to each other these days we end up arguing."

"Maybe you should see a marriage counselor."

"Too late. I just want out."

"But have you really thought this through? Maybe you haven't given yourself enough time with Jace. You married him about a month before I moved here, right? So you've only been together a year."

"Is that all?" Erica responded flippantly, examining her polished nails. "Seems longer."

"The first year's the most difficult, what with all the adjustments to make."

"I don't want to adjust. I'm so bored. I never imagined life on a ranch could be so damn dull."

"But Jace isn't dull."

"No, but now that I know what it's like to live out here in the sticks, I don't know how he can stand it day in and day out. After all, when he graduated from the naval academy he was stationed in some pretty exotic places. I don't know how he gave up all that excitement to come back here and take over the ranch when his father died."

"Traveling from place to place can get tiresome too, I imagine," Leah suggested quietly, cupping her coffee mug in both hands. "And Jace grew up on the ranch. It's home to him."

"Too bad home's in the middle of the boondocks."

A fleeting smile touched Leah's lips. "Well, you can't have a ranch in the middle of a city. Besides, we're not exactly cut off from civilization here."

"That's easy for you to say," Erica retorted with some impatience. "You don't mind driving twenty-five miles each way to your studio in Forth Worth and back every day, just to live the country life."

"Yes, that's why I bought this old place and fixed it up."

"And even filled that chicken coop in the back yard."

"I like having chickens around. My Uncle Billy always had them, and when I visited him I'd gather the eggs. I still like to do that. Besides, nothing's better than a fresh egg."

"I'd rather buy mine at a corner supermarket. Lord, it'll be nice to be close to stores and restaurants and entertainment again."

"You make it sound like Jace never takes you anywhere. I know he does."

"But we always come back here, and I've had enough. I need more excitement. If I don't get away soon, I'll go stir-crazy, I swear it."

"Where are you planning to go?"

"Vegas," Erica said with a flick of her wrist. "Land of the quick divorce. And I can get a job dancing in one of the revues. That's what I was doing when I first met Jace in Tahoe, you know."

"Yes," murmured Leah, thoughtfully swirling the coffee around in her mug. She hesitated a moment, then said, "Look, Erica, this isn't my business, but are you sure you're not making a big mistake? Jace is a fine man. He's intelligent and interesting. He has a great sense of humor and he's attractive."

"Sure, he's all of those things. But we just don't get along. It's over."

"Well, it's your decision. I just hope you don't regret it someday."

"I won't. Leah, I know you like Jace a lot."

"Yes, I do."

"He likes you too, you know."

"Good," Leah said flatly. A tiny frown appeared on her smooth brow. "I hope you're not insinuating that he and I..."

Erica laughed out loud. "Heavens no! You're not the type to covet your neighbor's husband. That would be too immoral. And good ol' Jace, he's just like you."

"I'm glad you realize that."

"Of course I do. I was just reminding you that you two are friends. So maybe if you were the one to tell him I've left, he'd—"

"I won't do it, Erica. Don't ask me to again," Leah declared tersely. She didn't appreciate Erica's attempts to manipulate her, although she had known for some time that Erica was basically a manipulative person. The woman came on friendly, and exuded charm. But she was always looking out for number one, even if that meant using other people. Leah had learned that early on about her neighbor. She hadn't seen as much of Erica lately as she had when she'd first moved in, and the truth of the matter was that she really didn't want to see Erica now. Leah wished she would go.

Fortunately, after a couple more minutes of idle chatter, Erica glanced at the diamond-studded gold watch on her wrist. She rose languidly to her feet. "I'd better go. Jace is out riding the range or poking the cows or whatever it is he does, but he usually gets back around six. I want to be gone before he comes in."

Leah escorted her to the back door. "Then you're not going to stay and talk to him? You're just going without a word?"

"Oh, I'll leave him a note." Erica smiled rather slyly. "Tell you what. Since you like Jace so much, he's all yours now. I'm giving him to you."

"I think Jace would have something to say about that. He's not yours to give," Leah replied stiffly. "He's his own man."

"Yeah, you're right. He is. That was part of the

problem, I guess. I have to admit I like to have a man I can twist around my little finger."

"You married the wrong one, then."

"I'll say." Erica stopped on the threshold to give Leah a brief, insincere hug, then kissed the air in the vicinity of her cheek. A deliberate miss. She was a woman who didn't want to smudge her lipstick. "See you."

"Good-bye," Leah responded with no regret. *Jace will be better off without you.* She didn't speak those words aloud. She knew the thought was uncharitable, but it was how she felt. And how was Jace going to feel when he came home tonight and found his wife had deserted him? Hoping with all her heart he wouldn't be too hurt, she stepped outside and went around the house to look across the road at the Austin ranch house, set back in a copse of oaks and cottonwoods. Erica was approaching the front door.

Leah turned away to gaze across her own back yard. Pecan trees and lush willows flourished along the small creek that meandered on a few more miles, to feed the bluegreen waters of the Brazos River. Patches of bluebonnets had sprung up here and there and their delicate blossoms swayed in the warm breeze. With a faint smile, Leah turned back to watch the white and mahogany Herefords grazing on the rolling grassland that was fenced in by barbed wire on either side of Jace's house. She couldn't really understand how anyone, even Erica, could willingly leave such natural beauty. To Leah, it meant peace and tranquillity. Taking a deep breath, she inhaled the sweet, fresh air.

Jace Austin found the note propped up on the

sink in the bathroom adjacent to the utility room, where he showered and changed clothes every evening before dinner. The note was short. He read it quickly, tossed it aside, and washed his hands before walking back outside and across the road to Leah's house. He went around to the side, knocked on the screen door, and smiled lazily when she appeared a few moments later.

"Evening, Leah," he said, removing his Stetson respectfully. "Erica left me a note telling me to come over here."

Leah's throat nearly squeezed shut. Her hands began to tremble and she clasped them together in front of her. "Is that all the note said?"

"That's it. Is she here?"

"I . . . well, no, she isn't."

"Do you know where she is then?"

"I—I . . ." At that moment she could have throttled Erica Austin and thoroughly enjoyed doing it. That woman had done this on purpose to embarrass Leah and humiliate Jace. Leah didn't want to tell him the truth, but here he was standing on her doorstep, a tall rangy man with a lean sun-bronzed face. There was a puzzled expression shaping his carved features. She had to tell him. She couldn't let him just wonder where his wife had disappeared to. Damn that Erica! Squaring her shoulders, Leah prepared herself for his reaction. "Erica left," she said as gently as possible. "She asked me to tell you but I didn't think it was my place. She—"

"I see," Jace interrupted, a hint of anger and disgust in his voice. "Did she happen to mention where she was going?"

Nodding, Leah regarded his expression. It told her nothing at all, gave no clue to his feelings. Was he the strong silent type that kept everything hidden inside? she wondered. Her heart went out to him as she murmured, "Las Vegas."

"I'm sure I'll be hearing from her. Thanks for the message." He turned away, shaking his head.

Leah watched him go, feeling utterly helpless.

Jace himself felt strange, torn by conflicting emotions. The end of any marriage is always traumatic. And he had always believed his marriage would last forever. But with Erica it hadn't worked out that way. They had never been right for each other, and deep inside he experienced the release of warm relief. They had discussed separation several times during the past few months, and now he wasn't really sorry that she had gone. It was the timing of her departure that surprised him, and the fact that she had left without a word. And, of course, being single again was going to take some getting used to.

One evening three weeks later, Jace saw Leah tending her vegetable garden. Tossing his Stetson onto a chair on his veranda, he walked across the road and up her driveway.

"Where have you been keeping yourself?" he asked as he approached. She glanced up at him, then down again quickly. A small frown creased his brow. "I'm getting the idea you've been avoiding me."

"Not really. Well, maybe I have," she admitted, rising to her feet and brushing away the soil that clung to the knees of her jeans. Her steady gaze met his. "I thought maybe you'd rather not see me for a while, since I was the one who told you that Erica left."

Jace's frown deepened. "I'm sorry she put you in that position. It was a rotten thing to do."

"Oh, don't worry about that. I just knew you must be pretty upset, and since I was the bearer of the bad tidings, I—"

"Not bad tidings, Leah," he interrupted softly, shaking his head. "I guess I should have told you the night you gave me the news. Erica and I had been talking about separating for quite a while. I'd already told her I thought she should leave. I just didn't think she'd do it so soon. Her timing was really all that surprised me."

Leah's dark green eyes widened. "You'd asked her to leave? The impression she gave me . . . well, never mind. I'm just glad you aren't upset. I thought—"

"That I was a poor deserted husband crying myself to sleep at night," he finished for her, his lazy smile crinkling the corners of his clear blue eyes. "I admit the past few weeks haven't been the best in my life. It's not easy to end a marriage, but I'm handling it."

"Well, I never imagined you crying into your pillow, but I did think you might be very hurt."

"And since you were the reluctant messenger you've been feeling guilty?"

"Well, very concerned. But that's all straightened out now. I'm relieved."

"Good. But I'm disappointed that you thought I was the kind of man to blame the messenger for bad news."

"Oh, that's not what I meant. I . . ." Leah broke off with a rueful smile as she recognized the teasing glimmer in his eyes. "I have a great idea. Why don't we just forget all about my misunderstanding the situation?"

"Done," he agreed. Taking a few steps toward her between the vegetable rows, he surveyed the entire garden. "Looks like you have a very green thumb. Everything you planted came up."

"I know. It's wonderful. Everything's growing like weeds except the weeds, thanks to you. If I hadn't taken your advice and put mulch between the rows, I'd probably be spending all my time weeding, and the plants wouldn't be nearly as healthy. Look at these," she said excitedly, indicating the tomato plants. "Have you ever seen so many blossoms? And some of the tomatoes have started forming. I'm going to have to move the ties up on the stakes before the tops start breaking off. How high do you think they might grow?"

"The way you're taking care of them, they'll probably reach five, six feet."

"And I'll have more tomatoes than I know what to do with. Guess I'll have to learn how to can vegetables whether I want to or not," she said wryly, going past him to start toward the house. "Come on in. I made a pitcher of fresh lemonade when I got home from the studio."

Silently accepting her invitation, he followed her into the airy yellow kitchen, where an appetizing aroma wafted from the oven. He sniffed appreciatively. "Something smells delicious."

"Thanks, but it's nothing fancy. Just a chicken roasting."

"I love roast chicken."

Taking the pitcher of lemonade from the refrigerator, Leah glanced over at him and smiled. "Would you like to stay for dinner?"

"Thought you'd never ask," he answered with an answering smile. "Since Erica left, I've been eating with the hands nearly every night. Cookie has two specialties, steak and potatoes and potatoes and steak. Very monotonous. I've decided to start cooking for myself again out of sheer self-defense."

"I hope you have more than two specialties."

"I have quite a few actually. I was a bachelor for a long time, so I had to learn to cook, or starve. I make great lasagna, for instance."

"Mmm, one of my favorites," she murmured, motioning him toward the table as she handed him a glass of lemonade. Then she sat down across from him. "Speaking of Erica, have you heard from her yet?"

"She called the day after she left to tell me she was going to file for divorce right away. It'll be final in about a month. Luckily the community property isn't going to be complicated. The only thing we acquired since we got married was the two hundred acres of extra grazing land I bought last fall. I'm giving her a cash settlement for her half."

Leah took a sip of lemonade. "Maybe you won't have to do that," she suggested softly. "Maybe the two of you can work things out and get back together."

Jace shook his head. "No. It's over. I'm surprised we stayed together nearly a year. Remember that old saying, 'marry in haste, repent at leisure'? It sure did apply to Erica and me. We met in Tahoe and got married two weeks later, without really knowing each other. I guess we thought we knew enough, but . . . I don't really know what I expected from her, but I think she'd been watching too much *Dallas*. She seemed to expect life on a Texas ranch to be as glamorous and as full of intrigue as it is on TV."

"We all have our little fantasies, I guess. And some people get married simply because they're lonely."

Gazing at her over the rim of his glass, Jace nodded. "I guess that's why I did."

"Then don't you miss Erica? No, forget I asked that. I'm sorry. It's none of my business," Leah said, twirling a lock of hair around one finger. "I didn't mean to sound nosy."

"You didn't. Just concerned. After all, you've known Erica and me almost as long as we've been married. You get involved with people you know—I understand that. But no, I don't think I miss Erica at all. You know how it is. Sometimes you can be lonelier living with someone you can't really get along with than you would be living by yourself."

"I can imagine. I'm just sorry it didn't work out."

"Me too. But I'm thirty-three, and getting married was the biggest mistake I've made so far. I can't complain, I guess." Jace took a long swallow of iced lemonade. "How old are you, Leah?"

"Twenty-six."

He raised his dark brown eyebrows. "That old?"

She laughed. "Well, don't make it sound so ancient."

"That's not what I meant. It's just that you look younger. A couple years at least."

Watching him rake his fingers through his thick dark hair, she continued to smile. "I'm not sure whether to take that as a compliment or an insult."

"Why would you think it might be an insult?"

"Well, I don't want to look too young."

"I thought all women wanted to look younger than they are."

"That's only after we reach a certain age. I haven't reached it yet."

"Lord, deliver me," he muttered comically, rolling his eyes heavenward in answer to her teasing grin. "Is there any man alive who really understands the way women think?"

"Oh come on, we're not that mysterious."

"Couldn't prove it by me. Ever been married, Leah?"

"Never even come close."

"Wise lady," he said, a scarcely discernible hint of bitterness in his deep voice. "Just remember not to rush into anything."

"I've always tried to be a cautious person," she assured him, getting up from the table. "The chicken should be ready. And I have some potato salad to go with it. Something cool for such a hot day. Of course, you might want to skip that, since your cook gives you potatoes all the time."

"Potato salad's different. Sounds great. Anything I can do to help?"

She opened a cabinet door. "Sure, you can set the table. The plates are in here. We'll have to eat in the kitchen—I haven't finished wallpapering the dining room."

"But you've done a lot with this old place. It really looks nice. When you first bought it, it was in pretty bad shape."

"At least it was structurally sound. That was the only good thing you could say about it. For the first couple of months after I moved in I wondered if I'd gotten in over my head. But it's been worth all the work to see it looking this good. And I want to thank you again for suggesting that I have insulation installed in the attic and blown into the walls. It was very cozy in here all winter, and it's cool now that the weather's hot."

"How are things going at the studio?" Jace asked when they sat down to dinner. "Business good?"

"Very good. Of course, Uncle Evan was one of the most popular photographers in Fort Worth, so when he retired and I bought the studio from him I had a ready-made clientele. I don't think I've lost any of his old regulars, and advertising has brought in new ones. I get lots of blushing brides and graduates. And, of course, babies and young children."

"Kids must be a challenge."

"That's a major understatement. Yesterday, I had a two-year-old boy in for a sitting and he wouldn't sit still. He was into everything, but I was finally able to get a few good shots of him."

"And I suspect you enjoyed every minute of it."

"Not every minute. He was a bit too rambunctious. But I do enjoy my work," Leah said. "It's rewarding to try to capture all the facets of people with a camera. It's so nice when my subjects relax and let me do that. If they're all tensed up, the photos don't come alive. You can't see the real person in them. One thing about that two-year-old yesterday, he wasn't tense. I have a feeling I'm going to see a devilish twinkle in his eyes when I develop the proofs on Friday."

"Now that you mention uptight subjects, some of my hands seemed self-conscious when you rode out with us to round up strays in April. Your camera made them a little edgy," Jace told her as he lifted a forkful of potato salad to his mouth. "How did the pictures turn out?"

"Terrific, for the most part. Some of the men were camera-shy, but I got some really great shots. I've been meaning to bring them over to show you but I never got around to it. Would you like to see them after we finish eating? There are several good ones of you."

"Don't see how," he drawled, a trace of a grin tugging at his firm lips. "I'm camera-shy too."

"Hah! I think you're something of a ham," she retorted with a knowing smile. "You don't look the least bit self-conscious in any of the shots. In fact, you're a natural, a photographer's dream. Just wait until you see yourself—a man and his horse out on the range, everybody's idea of what a real Texas rancher should look like."

"Dust on my boots and all?"

She nodded. "Down to the last detail."

During the remainder of the meal, they talked easily, one topic of conversation leading into another. They basically agreed on most things, but when they discussed a few of the books they had read recently, they parted company on one of them.

"I hated that book," Leah said frankly. "The author must despise women. He made the heroine, if you can even call her that, such a dreadful character that it seemed to me he made no attempt to give her any depth."

Jace raised his eyebrows. "What do we have here, a dyed-in-the-wool, militant women's-libber?"

"Not militant at all. I just think Larsen either got lazy and didn't bother to create a believable character, or he hates women."

"I agree that the heroine wasn't likable," Jace admitted, "but the plot was strong and he does have a way with words."

"Hitler had a way with words too," she replied. Then she returned Jace's easy smile, tacitly agreeing to disagree.

After stacking the dishes in the sink Leah led Jace into the living room, where she showed him the photos she had taken of him and his men on the range. He was silent as he slowly looked them over. At last he nodded his approval.

"These are very good, Leah. Ever thought about trying to win prizes for your work?"

"Oh my, yes. I used to daydream about winning at least one Pulitzer for photojournalism," she confessed. "I even worked for the Houston Chronicle for a while, hoping to catch that once-in-a-lifetime photo."

"Maybe you didn't wait long enough. Why did you quit the paper?"

"I stopped enjoying what I was doing after a while. I was a feature photographer, and newspaper editors seem to have a strange quirk. I'd send up a batch of pictures to go with a story and some editor would always choose the worst one for publication. Then I was the one who got the calls from the people in the pictures. They'd say, 'I'm not that fat,' or, 'I'm not that skinny,' or, 'I look like I have a million wrinkles in that awful picture you put in today's paper. Why did you have to pick that one? You must have taken some that didn't make me look so bad!'" Leah shrugged. "But that's not the real reason I quit. I didn't mind the minor hassles. What I did mind was the hectic pace of my life. I decided city life wasn't for me. So here I am. And I'm happier. Now I don't worry about getting that prize-winning shot. I just collect my favorite photos for my own enjoyment."

Jace's blue eyes narrowed slightly as he regarded her intently. "And no regrets, Leah?"

"Oh, a twinge once in a while, but I get over it," she replied, shrugging carelessly. "And what about you? Do you ever regret leaving the excitement of the navy to come back to the ranch?"

"Like you, I have a twinge now and then. But no, I'm not sorry I resigned my commission. I'm happier ranching," he said, gathering the photographs together in a neat stack on the coffee table and rising to his feet. "Do you mind if I borrow these for a few days so the men can see them?"

"Be my guest. If anyone wants a print, just let me know. No charge, of course. It's the least I can do, since some of them were such unwilling subjects."

Smiling, Jace inclined his head. "I'd better get going now. Thanks for dinner."

"Any time you get tired of steak and potatoes, come back over," she murmured, escorting him to the front door and across the screened-in porch. Dusk was falling, creating pools of shadow beneath the lush foliage of the oak trees in the yard. Leah stood on the threshold, holding the screen door open as Jace moved lightly down the steps. He turned back toward her, hesitating. Leah smiled at him faintly, and he came up the steps again to grasp the frame of the door just above her hand. His little finger brushed against hers.

"Would you do me a favor?" he asked softly, holding her puzzled gaze. "I'm having my yearly barbecue for the local ranchers on Saturday, but Sue, my sister, isn't going to be able to help me. She can't make it this weekend. She thought she could but . . . anyway, could you lend a hand?"

Leah sighed. "I wish I could, Jace, but I keep the studio open on Saturdays until noon, and I have several appointments booked."

"The barbecue won't start until midafternoon."

"Oh, then there's no problem."

"You're sure you don't mind?"

"Of course not," she said. "What are neighbors for? But how can I help?"

"Oh, just mingle mostly, and make sure everybody's having a good time. Nothing to it."

"What should I wear?"

"Something simple. Jeans or a dress if you want. It's not formal."

She breathed an exaggerated sigh of relief. "Good. I loaned my diamond tiara to a friend and I wouldn't think of going formal without it."

Low laughter rumbled deep in his throat as he nodded good night. "Thanks, neighbor. See you Saturday if not before."

"'Night, Jace," Leah called after him as he walked away, his strides long and easy. She closed and hooked the screen door and went back into the parlor. Shutting the solid oak front door, she leaned back against it. She knew Jace had asked for her help because Erica was gone. Leah wasn't sure he really believed he and Erica would never get back together again. Maybe he was only saying that because he was afraid to hope they might. But they were still married, and would be for the next three or four weeks. A reconciliation was still a possibility.

Leah wondered how he really felt.

CHAPTER TWO

The Texas sky was a lovely blue, scattered here and there with puffs of white cloud. The sun shone brightly, but a gentle breeze eased the heat of its rays. Perfect weather for a barbecue. Kept busy as hostess, Leah mingled and made sure the old-timers sitting in the shade of the cottonwood trees got all they wanted to eat and drink. Children scampered around the yard, some of them playing tag while others took turns on the swing hanging from a thick oak limb. Jace handled the barbecuing himself, bantering good-naturedly with the guests about his secret recipe for the sauce and refusing to tell any of them the ingredients he used to give it a spicy zest. From time to time Leah took a few minutes to get some photographs of the gathering.

She already knew most everyone who was there, and introduced herself to those she didn't know. Chatting with a young couple who lived on a nearby ranch, Leah glanced over at Jace and saw that he was trying to get her attention. He beckoned her to him with a crooked finger.

"Would you excuse me?" she said, and walked

over to the hot barbecue pit. She looked up at Jace. "You must be burning up, you've been standing here almost two hours. Why don't you let me take over for a while so you can cool off in the shade?"

"I'll take you up on that offer later," he said, handing her a ladle. "Right now, would you mind keeping an eye on the chili while I go inside and get another jug of iced tea and some more beer?"

She nodded, and smiled at two of the guests, who approached for second or perhaps third helpings of the beanless Texas-style chili.

"I'm telling you, it's using the right kind and just the right amount of tomatoes that makes all the difference in chili," one said to the other. "Jace knows that for a fact. That's why his is so good."

"Nope. It's the onions," the other insisted, nodding his thanks to Leah when she served him a generous portion. "Tomatoes are important but it's the onions that make the chili."

"Well, now, I think you're wrong as you can be . . ." "My daddy always said . . ."

The low-key debate continued as the men ambled away toward the trees. Leah was smiling to herself when a plump hand squeezed her shoulder.

"Haven't had a chance to say hello before now, you've been so busy," Hattie Briscoe announced, her smile warm and friendly. "It's mighty nice of you to help Jace out this way."

"I'm happy to do it. It's nice to see you again, Mrs. Briscoe."

"Oh, call me Hattie. Everybody does."

"Hattie then. How have you been?"

"Just fine. Busy, with the kids out of school, but at least Debbie's home from college for the summer, so she drives them when they want to go places. Gives me time to get my work done. That sure is a pretty dress you're wearing. That peach color looks so good with your hair. And before I forget, I have to tell you I can't believe how you've fixed up your house. It's amazing. From the outside it looks like a brand new place. How'd you get so much done so fast? You still have your studio in Fort Worth, don't you?" Hattie asked, hurrying right on when Leah nodded. "My son and his wife are coming to visit next week, bringing my new grandbaby. I'd like to get some pictures made of her while they're here. Do you think you might be able to fit us in?"

"Sure. Call me at the studio Monday and I'll see which appointments I can rearrange."

After expressing her thanks, Hattie moved closer to Leah as she stirred the simmering chili. "Tell me something. Where did Erica run off to?"

It was a question Leah had already heard a few times that day. She answered simply, "Las Vegas."

"Did she go off with another man?"

"No, I don't think so."

"Why did she run off then?"

"I don't know," was Leah's noncommittal answer. "I guess she had her reasons."

"I wonder what happened between her and Jace."

"That's something only the two of them know, I guess."

Hattie lowered her voice a little. "I have to tell you I wondered from the very start if she was right for him. I mean, she just didn't seem to fit into his life.

Now, I don't mean to sound like a gossip, it's just that I've always been fond of Jace, and I kind of hoped he'd get together with my Debbie. She's more his type, lived on a ranch all her life. But mothers can't choose for their children, and he's never been more than friendly to Debbie. She had a crush on him for a while but she's grown out of it. So that's that. Do you think Erica might come back to Jace?"

"She could, I suppose," Leah said softly. "Anything's possible."

"I think Jace is better off without her. And he doesn't seem to be too upset that she's gone."

"Sometimes it's not easy to tell what other people are really feeling."

"That's right, but I know Jace, and I think if he wanted her back he'd go to Las Vegas and haul her home. He'd at least try to keep her," Hattie said knowingly. "When he wants something, he goes after it. His daddy was the same way. All the Austin men I know are—"

"What, Hattie?" Jace asked as he stepped up behind them, giving them a slow smile. "What about us Austin men?"

"You all make the best chili to be found," Hattie replied earnestly, giving his right arm a pat. "Your cousin Bobby makes the best in Denton County and you make the best here. But don't tell Henry I said that. He'll think I'm being a very disloyal wife. Well, I see Mary Lou Barker waving at me. I'd better go talk to her."

As Hattie left them, Jace tipped Leah's chin up with one lean finger, his eyes looking into hers. He smiled gently. "What did she really tell you about Austin men?"

"Nothing, except that you make great chili."

"*Leah*."

"You don't need to know what else she said," she told him, wrinkling her nose mischievously. "We women like to have our little secrets."

"Oh? Well I hope she didn't tell you about some of my youthful escapades."

"Were you a wild teenager?"

"I'll just let you wonder about that. I can have secrets too," he said wryly, taking the ladle from her hand. "Have you eaten yet?"

"I've been nibbling all afternoon. Everything's delicious, but I really don't need another bite."

"Looks like everybody's slowing down," Jace said, looking around. He dropped the ladle back in the pot and went to a nearby pecan tree to get a cold can of beer from the ice filled tub standing in the shade. He took a long swallow and leaned back against the tree, one foot propped behind him against the trunk. "It does feel good to get away from that fire."

As twilight fell, someone turned on music and people began to dance to the mellow strains of country-and-western ballads. The dark yard remained in shadow even after Jace turned on some outdoor lights. Overhead, the stars were big and sparkling in the velvet canopy of the sky and a half moon shone down brightly. Leah danced with a couple of the unattached men and then was claimed by Henry Briscoe, Hattie's husband. He was as quiet as she was talkative, speaking only a few words to Leah before Jace politely asked to cut in. With a nod Henry drifted off into the shadows.

"He's a nice man. A little shy, I think," Leah commented. She rested her hands on Jace's broad shoulders as his arms lightly slipped around her waist. "Or is he one of those lone cowboy types?"

"I think he's just quiet. Could be a little shy, though," Jace speculated. "I wonder if was hard for him to get up the nerve to ask Hattie for that first date."

"Maybe she asked him."

"Could very well be. I doubt Hattie's ever been one to let grass grow around her feet. If Henry was too shy to get things started, I imagine she took matters into her own hands. When she wants something, she can be a very determined woman."

"That's a coincidence. She said the same thing about you."

"What? That I could be a very determined woman?"

Leah laughed. "No, that you're willing to go after what you want. Somehow she made you sound a little dangerous."

"Why? You're the kind of person to go after what you want too. If you weren't, you wouldn't have worked so hard renovating your house. That doesn't make you seem dangerous to me," Jace said softly. "You haven't lived here long enough to realize this part of the country requires perseverance. It's a virtue. Do I still seem a little dangerous?"

"No," Leah murmured, although she was not so sure that was true. Then the music faded, and Leah stepped away from Jace. "You'd better dance with some of the other ladies. They might feel neglected."

"Can't have that," Jace agreed, and left her.

A few hours later the guests started to leave. Some of them had fairly long drives home. By eleven o'clock only the Briscoes remained—they lived just five miles away. Henry yawned once, and again almost immediately. Hattie chuckled.

"I can take a hint, honey. We'll go now," she said, scooting her two youngest children toward the family station wagon. Hattie went over to give Jace a quick peck on the cheek. "Had a lovely time as usual." She turned to Leah, who was standing nearby as Debbie and Henry said good night to Jace. "Now, we're having our barbecue three weeks from today. Jace already knows I expect him to be there, but I want you to promise to come too," she told Leah.

"I wouldn't miss it."

After all the good nights were exchanged, the Briscoes drove away. Leah suddenly found herself remarking, "Debbie is a very pretty girl."

"She's turning into a handsome woman. Nice, too," Jace responded casually.

Leah tapped a fingertip against her lips. His tone of voice reflected genuine fondness, but no hint of romantic interest. Despite her wishes to the contrary, Hattie was apparently right—Debbie and Jace were probably destined to be no more than friends.

"Leah." Jace quietly spoke her name. "Penny for your thoughts."

"They aren't worth that much," she said, rousing herself from her reverie. She smiled at him. "Well, this was some shindig. I really enjoyed it. But now it's time to clean up."

"I'll make sure all the coals are out while you take what's left of the food inside," he said, heading toward the barbecue pit. "There should be plenty of room in the refrigerator."

There was. There was some food left over, but not much. The ranch hands had feasted heartily, apparently as weary as Jace was of Cookie's unimaginative menu.

After finishing in the kitchen, Leah went back outside. Jace was still covering the faintly glowing embers. Rain had been scarce the past few weeks and one wayward spark could ignite the dry grass disastrously. She went over to sit in the swing suspended from the sturdy oak tree, watching as he shoveled dirt over the bed of coals. In the dim light she saw the rippling of his shoulder muscles as his tan shirt strained against him each time he bent over. She looked away, confused by her reaction to the sight of him.

"That does it," he announced a few minutes later, coming over to the swing. Grasping the wooden seat, he pulled her back, gave a push, and sent her arcing up into the air.

"Oh this is nice," she called to him. The mingling fragrances of wild honeysuckle and cultivated jasmine perfumed the night, and she closed her eyes and rode the arcs as he pushed her again and again.

After a while he caught the ropes of the swing and held her still. "Look up," he commanded softly. "I don't think I've ever seen so many stars out."

She sighed contentedly. "It is a beautiful night."

"There's nothing like a Texas sky."

"Some people would disagree with you."

"Then they've never seen a Texas sky at midnight."

"Or you're just prejudiced."

"Hmm, could be."

A light tremor ran up Leah's spine. She had swept her hair forward across one shoulder to expose her warm nape to the cool air, and now she felt the light caress of Jace's breath upon her skin. It tickled and tingled and made her heart beat a bit too fast for comfort. She slipped off the swing, planting her feet firmly on the ground.

"I should get home now."

"I'll walk you over."

"Oh, you don't have to."

He insisted. "My parents raised me to be the epitome of a country gentleman, and gentlemen always see a lady to her door."

Grinning, she gave him a curtsy. "How gallant you are, sir."

"Never say chivalry is dead," he retorted, taking her elbow as he escorted her across the road.

Knowing she'd be late getting home, Leah had left the front light on. Inside the screen porch, she looked up at Jace. The soft glow of the overhead bulb accentuated the rich copper tone of his skin. His darkening blue eyes slowly explored her upturned face. There was a funny sensation in her chest. "Well, good night," she murmured, turning toward her front door.

"Leah," he said quietly, one large hand on her shoulder turning her back to him, his other cupping her chin. "Thanks for the help."

She tried to give him a matter-of-fact smile, but it trembled on her lips as he lowered his head to kiss her cheek gently. She could feel the heat emanating from his long lithe body. Or was that simply her imagination? She couldn't be sure. Yet imagination had nothing to do with the clean woodsy scent of his aftershave. That was very real and very appealing. Her breath caught as he stepped closer to her and she wanted him to kiss her again. But an instant before his warm, strong mouth grazed over the softness of hers, danger signals went off wildly in her head. Heeding the intuitive warning, she gracefully spun around on one heel, opened her door, and stepped across the threshold. "Good night, Jace," she managed to say steadily.

Jace called Leah Wednesday evening. "How about a movie and dinner tonight?" he asked. "I know it's short notice. Have you already made plans?"

"Well, I—"

"Don't tell me you have to wash your hair."

She laughed. "If I was going to make up an excuse, I'd try to think of something a little more original than that."

"Would you like to go then?"

She hesitated only a moment before saying, "Yes, I'd love to go. What movie did you have in mind?"

"There are a few playing in Fort Worth that sound interesting. We can decide which one to see on the way. We could have dinner first, and go to the nine o'clock show. Can you be ready by six thirty?"

"Sure."

"Okay. See you then."

After Leah hung up, she hurried into her bedroom to wash up and apply some makeup before going through her closet and choosing something to wear.

At six thirty on the dot Jace knocked on her door. When she opened it he seemed somewhat surprised to find her with purse in hand.

"I thought I'd have to wait for you," he admitted, his gaze drifting over her sleeveless blue dress. "I didn't know any woman could get ready to go out in just half an hour."

"I've had to learn how to get going fast, because I'm a chronic oversleeper," she confessed, locking her door on the way out. "Most mornings I shut off the alarm and turn back over, hiding my head under the pillow. Then when I finally manage to drag myself out I have to run around like mad to make it to the studio on time. I think my record is getting up, dressed, and out the door in ten minutes."

"That must be a sight to see."

"A pitiful one. A grown woman should be able to get herself out of bed early enough in the mornings."

"Nobody's perfect. We all have our little failings."

"You too? Give me an example."

"I talk in my sleep sometimes," Jace said, opening the passenger door of his white Volvo for her. "Luckily, I've never revealed any of my deepest secrets that way. What I say doesn't make any sense—or so I've been told."

"That's not so terrible. My father snores very loudly. Mother says he sounds like a foghorn."

Smiling, Jace walked around the car and slipped in behind the steering wheel. He started the engine and pulled out onto the road, smoothly changing gears as they picked up speed. "Your folks live near Austin, don't they?"

"Uh-huh. That reminds me, I've been meaning to ask you if you're related to the Austins the city was named for."

"My Aunt Ellie swears we're cousins of old Moses Austin," he said wryly as he settled himself more comfortably in his seat. "But even she admits we're something like fourteenth cousins twenty times removed. Nobody else in the family claims kinship."

"Maybe you should. You look like you come from pioneer stock, lean and rugged. The strong determined set of your jaw," Leah said lightly, chuckling when he jutted out his chin in the comically exaggerated attitude of a frontiersman.

Dinner was delicious, the adventure movie entertaining, and it was after eleven when they left the outskirts of Fort Worth behind. The road stretched out before them, and slipping off her shoes, Leah tucked her feet up beside her for the long ride home.

"I thought I might get tired of driving all this way back and forth from the studio every day," she told Jace, "but so far I haven't."

"Probably because you've lived in Texas all your life. Here, it seems like you just naturally have to go a long way to get from one place to the next."

"Ah, but I didn't live on a ranch. Our house is in the country, but only about six miles from Austin."

"Then I guess you've proved you have some of that frontier spirit yourself by buying your place. How'd your folks like the idea of your doing that? Were they worried about you being so far from town?"

"Dad seemed to think I was going out into the wilderness alone, never to be heard from again, but I managed to reassure him. Then they came to see me last fall and Mom was appalled by the condition of the house. She was afraid I'd never survive in winter, so I've been easing her mind by sending her pictures of all the improvements I've made since. Now they just accept the fact that I like living there, but I don't think they understand why. And my sister thinks I'm nuts. Lynn likes the excitement of the city. She and her husband live in a very nice apartment in Dallas. For sisters, we're not much alike."

"Is she older or younger than you?"

"One year older."

"Sue's eight years younger than me. My folks had to wait a long time for a second child."

"Tell me about them," Leah asked gently. "At the barbecue I heard so many nice things said about them."

"They were nice people. Made for each other. Even after I grew up I'd catch them necking in the parlor once in a while," Jace said, a reminiscent smile touching his lips. "Aunt Ellie used to tell them all that hugging and kissing in front of Sue and me would be a bad influence—she sure had some wacky notions. Knowing how much they loved each other always made me feel secure. They really needed each other. Ma died about two years after I graduated from Annapolis, and Dad was never the same. He passed away less than three years after she did."

"I guess Sue was still in school then. Is that why you came back home?"

"I knew I would eventually, anyway. By that time, I had decided I didn't want to make the navy my career."

"It must have been hard for you—being responsible for Sue and the ranch all at once."

"Sue says I was very bossy back then, but we actually got along fine. She was a champ, very mature, and that made it easier for both of us. She was almost nineteen, so she was too old to be a brat, and since she was in college she was more or less independent. I didn't really boss her around. There were just times when we didn't agree on things she wanted to do, like drop out of school. Now she's glad I wouldn't let her. She called me a few nasty names and pouted for a day or two at the time, but we got through it."

"Didn't you tell me she teaches school?"

"Fourth grade. She loves kids."

"Have any of her own?"

"Not unless she's keeping a big secret from me," Jace quipped. "She's not married. Says she hasn't come close to finding the right man. She's very choosy." He glanced over at Leah. "Is that why you've never thought of getting married? Are you choosy too?"

"Yes," she answered flatly. "Especially where men are concerned."

"Meaning you don't trust us?"

"Meaning I don't trust some of you."

"What about me?"

"You seem trustworthy enough," she said, her tone light. "But then I don't know you all that well, do I?"

"Well, we'll have to do something about that," Jace replied. Reaching for her hand, he brought it down onto his right thigh, near his knee. Her heart seemed to do a wild little somersault and she started to pull her hand back, but as his fingers brushed lightly over hers, Leah found she didn't want to.

Twenty minutes later they arrived at Leah's house. Jace took the key from her and unlocked the front door. She smiled at him. "Thanks for a lovely evening,

Jace. I really enjoyed it."

As they stood in the screen porch, his hand grazed across her shoulder to curve around her nape beneath her hair. "I enjoyed it too, but it's not over quite yet."

Slowly, he bent down, and her lips parted in anticipation. More than anything in the world, she wanted to feel the touch of his lips, but there was something else to consider. Placing her palms lightly against his chest, she shook her head.

"Jace, I don't think we should let this happen. If you and Erica get back together, you and I might feel uncomfortable with each other about it. I wouldn't want that."

"Erica's not coming back. She doesn't want to and I don't want her to," he said firmly. "And I need to kiss you. You have a beautiful mouth."

"But, Jace, I—"

"Relax," he whispered, tipping her jaw up with the ball of his thumb. "Let me kiss you."

She could resist neither his coaxing words nor the first brushstroking contact with his lips. His mouth feathered over hers, probing her softness and causing tingling sensations to wash through her in a tender tide. Leah stepped closer to him as his arms went around her. Her hands were between them, pressed against his chest, and she could feel his warmth through the cotton fabric of his shirt. She stretched up on her toes, allowing her fingers to slide over his shoulders.

"Leah," he muttered against her mouth, increasing his embrace as he drew her nearer. Her slight curvaceous body felt good against his, and she tasted like heady wine. Aroused, he lifted her off her feet to hold her tightly against him.

He took her breath away. Her heart hammered, and for a few delightful moments all her natural sensuality held sway. His mouth was warm and gently possessive, and when his kiss deepened she felt almost dizzy.

Jace released her for a moment, only to pull her right back into his tight embrace and kiss her again and again.

And again. Leah kissed him back, content with the closeness they were sharing. But when his palms brushed across her to cup the straining sides of her breasts, she realized he might be expecting more from her than she was willing to give. Never a tease, she gained control of herself and reluctantly dragged her lips from his. For an instant she turned her face into the hollow of his shoulder, breathing in his clean scent. Then she stepped out of his arms, her gaze holding his. She shook her head. "I think you better go now."

"Leah," he began, unwilling to let her go. He touched her cheeks, her hair, his expression hopeful, until he saw the answer he didn't want to see in her eyes. Taking a deep breath, he gave her a boyish smile. "I don't suppose you'd consider inviting me to spend the night."

"You're right." She grinned back. "I wouldn't."

He cocked his head to one side. "Thought not. But you can't blame a man for trying."

"'Night, Jace," she said, still smiling as she opened the door and went inside.

He walked back to his car and got in. Leah seemed to be everything he had hoped to find in

Erica, but hadn't. Leah was definitely sweeter, wittier, and far more intriguing. She had a warmth and a capacity for giving that he liked very much. As he turned the key in the ignition Jace began to whistle, for the first time in a long time.

CHAPTER THREE

"Benjamin, move a little closer to your sister." Leah spoke to the five-year-old boy patiently as she focused the camera, but her instructions were futile. "No, don't move that light, Benjamin. I put it there to get a really good picture. Don't move it."

Benjamin Tibbets didn't listen. He rolled the standing light over to the side of the room and smiled with satisfaction.

Heaving a silent sigh of frustration, Leah went to retrieve the light. She usually had a great talent for handling children, but these two were proving to be real pips. And their mother, who stood observing the chaotic scene, showed no sign of wanting to intervene. After repositioning the light, Leah gently grasped the ceaselessly moving Benjamin by the shoulders and guided him back behind the settee, where his equally active sister sat swinging her legs.

"Now, please stand right here and don't move. Put this hand over the back of the chair. Lisa, you'll have to stop kicking your feet. Just be very quiet, both of you."

The children's mother finally spoke up. "Do what

the nice lady says. You want these to be pretty pictures, don't you?"

"Nope," Benjamin retorted.

"Nope," three-year-old Lisa parroted.

"Well, we're going to get some good ones anyway," Leah told them as she moved back behind her camera. Just as she got it focused again, Lisa slid off the settee, plopped down onto the floor, and started to unbuckle one of her patent leather Mary Janes.

"Please don't take your shoes off, Lisa," Leah said as lightly as possible. She picked up the little girl and put her back on the settee. "You'd look funny in the picture wearing just your socks."

"That's right, honey," Mrs. Tibbets added. "And don't sit on the floor, you'll get your dress dirty."

"Pretty," Lisa said, ignoring the parental advice as she ran a hand over Leah's hair. "Pretty."

"Thank you." Leah smiled, but the smile quickly faded as a strand somehow got caught in the clasp of the gold bracelet the child wore on her chubby right arm. Lisa made things worse by twisting her hand. Unable to straighten up, Leah tried to extricate herself but to no avail. She stood Lisa up on the settee and knelt beside her. "No, baby, don't pull. Let me try to get it out. Mrs. Tibbets, would you please come over here and take the bracelet off Lisa's arm. That might help."

"Need any assistance?" a deep voice asked from the doorway.

Glancing sideways, Leah saw Jace leaning against the doorjamb observing the scene.

"Oh, dear, I can't get the clasp open," Mrs. Tibbets murmured helplessly. "Don't wiggle your arm so much, Lisa. You're just making more of a tangle."

"Let me see what I can do," Jace suggested, going to the settee.

His hands were gentle, his fingers deft. To Leah's great relief, he soon freed her. "Thanks," she said, gingerly rubbing her scalp. "You couldn't have picked a better time to show up."

"Glad to be of service. I came to town on business and decided to stop by and see your studio."

"I'll show you around as soon as I'm finished here. Want to wait in my office?"

"I'd rather stay here and see the photographer at work, if that wouldn't bother you."

"Not at all. Take a chair." Leah proceeded to pose the children one more time, taking care to steer clear of Lisa's bracelet, which her mother had put back on the little girl's wrist. Behind her camera once more, she refocused and held her right arm out.

"Don't look straight at me. Look at my hand." She wiggled two fingers. "Think of Bugs Bunny. 'Eh, what's up, Doc,'" she mimicked. Luckily Benjamin and Lisa gave spontaneous and simultaneous smiles and she got several good shots in quick succession.

"The hard part's over, Mrs. Tibbets. It's not easy to get a picture of more than one child. Usually, one is smiling but the other one isn't, or one of them moves. It'll be easier to get shots of them individually. Benjamin, while I take some pictures of Lisa by herself you can play with the toys on that little table in the corner."

When he headed for the toys, his sister followed. Leah brought Lisa back and teased away the stormy expression that had appeared on her face. Still, it wasn't all smooth sailing after that.

"Lisa, take your thumb out of your mouth.... No, I don't want you to move your legs. Keep them crossed the way I showed you.... Just one more like that. Fold your hands in your lap, honey. That's it." Leah had to keep up a steady stream of encouragement and instruction while changing backgrounds and rearranging the lighting.

"All right. Last one, Lisa. Smile for me. Look at the man. Jace, please do something funny."

He obligingly made a crazy face. Lisa giggled. Leah snapped the shot with a satisfied grin. "Okay, you looked very pretty, Lisa. You can go play with the toys. It's Benjamin's turn."

"I wanna finish the puzzle," the little boy grumbled as Leah lead him in front of the camera. "And I'm tired of standing up."

"You're going to get to sit down this time."

"I'm hot."

"This won't take long."

"Mommy, I don't want to wear this anymore." Benjamin promptly removed his clip-on bow tie. "Do I have to?"

"Yes. Grandma wants pictures of you all dressed up."

Leah put the tie back on, straightened his collar, then managed to joke away his scowl.

Twenty minutes later, the session was over. After paying a deposit, Mrs. Tibbets left with the children, promising them they'd stop for ice cream if they were nice in the car.

As Leah breathed a loud sigh of relief, Jace smiled at her. "Quite a handful, weren't they?"

She gave him a look that spoke volumes. "They've been in for a sitting before and were very cooperative. I guess this just wasn't one of their better days."

"I'd say that's an understatement."

She smiled at him. In his gray pin-striped suit, he looked quite attractive. His white shirt accentuated the bronze of his skin, and the knot of his burgundy tie drew attention to the strong column of his neck. But it was his eyes her gaze lingered on. The shade of gray he wore deepened the aqua hue of his eyes, which met hers steadily.

"Ah, well, it's all in a day's work," she replied, glancing away from him for a second. "Thanks again for saving me from that bracelet. I don't know how it got so tangled up. I guess the clasp must have been open a little and since my hair's too fine anyway—"

"Not too fine," he murmured, reaching out to lift a golden strand. "It's beautiful and soft and silky. I like to touch it."

His knuckles brushed her cheek, accelerating her heartbeat. "Jace," she began.

"*Leah*," he countered, leaning down.

His kiss landed softly on her lips and its effect on her equilibrium was far too strong. Before she could succumb to the temptation he offered, Leah stepped back, shaking her head.

His dark brows raised questioningly.

"Jace, I was just starting to say that I still think we shouldn't get involved like this."

He looked at her intently. "Meaning you're simply not interested?"

"I didn't say I wasn't interested," she admitted, unable and unwilling to lie to him. "It's just that I . . ."

"You still think Erica and I might get back together? If you do, you're wrong."

"I know you mean it when you say that won't happen, and I think it probably won't."

"What's the problem then?"

"You're still a married man," she said quietly. "That's the problem."

He shook his head. "I'm a legally separated man. There's a big difference. And the divorce will be final in less than three weeks, so there's no problem, Leah."

"There is for me." She opened her hands expressively. "Let me explain something to you. My mother drilled it into my sister and me that we should never get involved with married men, and I agree with her. I just wouldn't feel right if we did."

A flicker of impatience crossed his face and quickly passed away. There was no use pressing her, he realized. That would get him nowhere. He inclined his head. "If that's the way you want it."

"That's the way I think it has to be."

"That's the way it will be then," he said quietly, allowing the tendril of her hair to trail out of his fingers. "How about that tour of the studio now?"

"All right." Hesitating, she touched his arm. "Jace, I want us to be friends."

"We are friends," he replied. "Now, the tour."

She immediately began to show him around, yet as she explained her work she felt tension gathering between them. Leah could only attribute it to the fact that their strong attraction to each other was out in the open. Maybe she should have lied to him—pretended she wasn't romantically interested. If she had, maybe they could have maintained an easy friendship. As it was now, she wasn't sure they could ever have it back the way it had been.

When Jace answered the phone Sunday morning, it was Leah calling.

"Something got one of my chickens last night," she said, the distress she felt strong in her voice. "One of them's missing, and there's blood and tracks outside the coop. I thought you might be able to tell what it was."

"I'll be right over."

"Thanks, Jace. I'll meet you outside."

Five minutes later, they walked down the gentle slope behind the house to the chicken coop. Jace took one look and nodded. "Just as I thought. It's a fox."

"But how did he get in? I remember shutting the gate."

"Must be a hole in the fence somewhere. Most of this chicken wire needs to be replaced. It was here years before you bought the place and it's rusting away," he said, walking around the perimeter of the coop. At one of the back corners, he stopped and showed her the hole the fox had used. "We can patch it and get a new fence up as soon as possible, but the fox will probably come back, and he may find another way in before we can do that."

"I don't want a damn fox carrying off my chickens," she said angrily. "Isn't there something I can do to protect them until I replace the wire?"

"Can you handle a gun?"

"A gun! Oh no, I'd probably shoot myself in the foot or something if I tried to fire one."

"I can send one of the hands over here tonight. If

the fox comes back, he can get him."

"Kill him, you mean?"

"That would put a stop to his midnight snacks."

Leah winced. "Well, I wasn't thinking of killing him."

"Unless you want to keep providing him chicken dinner every night, you'll have to do something. We could try a trap, lure him into a box with a spring door, then take him away, and let him go somewhere else," Jace suggested, amusement gentling his features. "Unless you want to try to tame him and keep him as a pet, since you're so tenderhearted."

She stuck her tongue out at him. "I'm not that tenderhearted. I just don't like to see any animal killed. Unless it's a snake. The only good snake is a dead one."

"On a ranch, or even if you just keep chickens, other animals can be more dangerous than snakes."

"But not as creepy."

"Maybe not, but sometimes they have to be killed."

"I guess so. But let's try the trap before we think about bringing out the guns."

"Okay. I can rig something up by tonight. Just let me fill this hole with some rocks for now."

"Thanks for the help," she said as they started back up the slope. "How about a cup of coffee before you go?"

"Sounds good," he agreed, following her into the house.

In the kitchen, she motioned him to the table as she took another mug out of the cabinet. "Black, right?"

"Yes," he answered, watching her move. She was still in her nightgown and a matching cotton robe, and there was a lingering drowsiness in her soft green eyes. As she came near him, he smiled. "I have a feeling you had a hard time getting up again this morning."

"What makes you think that? Just because I'm so bleary-eyed?" she wryly retorted. "I'm never going to win a prize for being an early riser. Faulty metabolism."

To him, there seemed to be nothing faulty about her, certainly nothing visible. Padding around in her slippers, she looked warm and cuddly. When she stepped beside him to pour the steaming coffee into his mug, he smelled the faint fragrance of her perfume, fresh and clean and inviting. The moment she put the percolator down on the counter, he caught hold of her hand, pulled her onto his lap, and kissed her.

His mouth captured her swift gasp of surprise. Caught off guard, she was unable to mount an initial defense against him and surrendered at once to the physical and emotional delight he aroused in her. She wound her arms around his neck as he held her tighter, her breasts yielding to the hard contours of his chest.

Holding her felt so good. The fresh scent of her hair and her slender shapely body enthralled him. Passion gathered in a throbbing ache in his loins and her every movement only heightened Jace's desire. His lips exerting a slight twisting pressure, he kissed her again and again, and she freely kissed him back.

He tenderly pushed the tip of his tongue into her

mouth and she met it eagerly with her own. Lost in the sensual excitement of the moment, Leah pressed closer, opening her mouth to the persuasive insistence of his, caressing the rims of his ears as his hands roamed over her back, setting her skin afire through the sheer fabric of her gown and robe.

"Leah," he murmured, tracing the delicate bone structure of her spine with his fingertips, "you want this as much as I do."

"Yes," she whispered. It was useless to try to lie to either him or herself. He drew her tongue more deeply in over his and her fingers tangled feverishly in the thick, dark hair grazing his nape.

Kisses weren't enough for him. He ached for more. His hands found the soft rising of her breasts and he cupped their weight in his palms. Then his thumbs explored her nipples, arousing them to sweet, firm buds.

Pleasure rocketed through her, keen and breathtaking. *Too* keen and breathtaking. Liking him, respecting him, attracted to him, she had allowed things to go too far. As his hands on her breasts became more possessively caressing, she dragged herself back to her senses.

"No, Jace," she murmured.

"*Leah.*"

"Don't. I can't. We said we . . ."

He groaned softly but released her. "Just friends, I know. I agreed to that, but God, woman, you—" Raking his fingers through his hair, Jace stood. "I think I'd better just get out of here, since I can't seem to keep my hands off you."

"Jace, I—"

"I'll have one of the hands bring the trap over when it's ready," he said. Then he was gone.

Still shaken by the depth of passion that had erupted between them, she went out to the screen porch to watch him cross the road. She wanted to call him back, but knew what might happen if she did. If he touched her again, she was afraid she might melt and abandon all resistance. Leah wasn't ready to let that happen. Their friendship was too important to her to be abandoned lightly for the sake of physical attraction. Yet how could that friendship remain unstrained now that their mutual attraction was out in the open?

Leah saw Jace only from a distance during the next two weeks. They exchanged waves across the road from time to time. She tried to tell herself it was better that way, but such logic didn't make her one whit happier about the situation. She missed seeing him, talking to him, and wondered if he missed her at all. He certainly wasn't making any effort to seek her company. Even when the fox had gone after the bait three nights after the trap was set, Jace had sent his foreman, Buddy, over to get the chicken thief and take him miles away to be released. Since he hadn't come himself, Leah had sent him her thanks through Buddy. Their deliberate avoidance of each other made her all the more tense. She was beginning to wonder if he was ever going to come see her, or even call again. And as the days and weeks passed she found it increasingly difficult to consider approaching him. They seemed to be locked in a stalemate, which was no way for neighbors to live, but she didn't know quite what to do about it. So she waited, hoping he would make the first move. If he didn't soon, she decided, she would.

She didn't have to. Jace called Monday evening, only minutes after she got home from the studio.

"Stop. Don't take that TV dinner out of the freezer yet," he drawled. "Have dinner here instead."

"Just give me time to freshen up and I'll be right over," she replied, pleased by the invitation. "I wasn't too thrilled by the tuna salad I planned to have, so thanks for asking."

"My sister's here for a visit and she wants to meet you."

That admission let some of the air out of Leah's balloon. Obviously he wouldn't have called if Sue wasn't there. But at least it was a step in the right direction. At least they would see each other. And surely there didn't have to be tension between them, did there? They were adults; they should be able to smooth things over. Wanting to believe that, she told him she'd be over as soon as she changed out of her linen suit into something even cooler.

Ten minutes later Leah met Sue Austin and liked her immediately. Like Jace, she was open and honest and not the least bit pretentious. She even resembled him a little. Her hair wasn't quite as dark, more a lustrous chestnut, with gold highlights, but her eyes were the same blue as his and just as warm and intelligent. Welcoming Leah at the front door, Sue led her into the living room. "Sit down. Jace is out talking to Buddy about branding the calves but he'll be in soon. I hoped to meet you when I was here at Christmas, but you were spending the holidays with your family, I believe."

"Yes. I'm sorry I missed you."

"How do you like living in the old Henderson place?" Sue asked as she took the chair across from the sofa where Leah sat. Smiling, she gestured to dismiss the idea. "I guess I shouldn't call it that anymore, should I?"

Leah smiled back. "I don't mind. I think folks around here will always think of it as the old Henderson place."

"Stick around for twenty years or so and they may start referring to it as the Bancroft place," Sue replied, laughing. "Whatever they call it, you've done an incredible job fixing it up. The outside looks great and Jace says you've done wonders inside too."

"I'm in the process of trying. I still have some painting and wallpapering to do. I hope to finish by fall. But if you'd like to take a look at the progress I've made so far, come over anytime. How about tomorrow evening?"

"Oh, I'd love to," Sue said, wrinkling her nose, "but I have to visit Aunt Ellie while I'm here, so Jace and I are having dinner with her tomorrow night. I love her, but she does go on and on sometimes about us being related to Moses Austin."

Leah grinned. "Jace told me about that. I'm impressed. Should I curtsy?"

"A simple bow from the waist will suffice," Sue retorted, managing to sound haughty until her laughter bubbled out. "Anyway, I do want to see what you've done to the house. I'm not flying back to Atlanta until Thursday, so maybe I could come over Wednesday night."

"I only keep the studio open half a day on Wednesdays. Come over in the afternoon if you like," Leah said. "Wear old clothes—I might even put you to work."

"Okay with me. I owe you one anyway. I thought I'd be able to make it to the barbecue but I couldn't get away. Jace told me you were kind enough to help him out. Thanks."

"What are neighbors for?" Leah responded, her voice lowering slightly as she glanced down at her hands in her lap. "I didn't realize you lived in Atlanta," she said, to change the subject. "Why so far from home?"

"I went to school there and loved it enough to stay. Besides, I wanted to be independent and give Jace some freedom. You see, we'd lost Ma and Dad both by the time I was nineteen and Jace took over a lot of responsibilities."

"Jace told me. I'm sorry," Leah said compassionately. "He also told me you teach school. I guess you're enjoying your summer vacation."

"If you can call it that. I'm running a summer reading program." Sue responded as Jace strode into the room. His hair was still damp from the shower he had taken and he was dressed informally in tan slacks and a pale blue rugby-style shirt with the collar open. Sue stood up. "Good, you're ready for dinner. I'll have you know I drove all the way to Fort Worth to buy fresh shrimp for scampi, because I know it's one of your favorites. I'll go check on it. Be back in a minute."

Left alone to play host to Leah, Jace walked over to the liquor cabinet across the room. "Blackberry wine?" he offered over his shoulder. "Home brew with

55

a little bit of a kick to it."

"I'd love some," said Leah. She rose from the sofa to join him, watching him pour the dark sparkling wine into three glasses. Then his magnificent blue eyes met hers and tension gathered like a cloud around the two of them. She hated it. Compulsively, she laid her fingers on his, her touch lingering too long simply because she enjoyed the feel of his skin. "Jace, can't we—"

"Don't start something you're not prepared to finish," he muttered abruptly, moving back a step to break contact. "I don't think you really want to come across as a tease."

"A tease?" she exclaimed softly, jerking her chin up a fraction of an inch as angry resentment washed over her. "You, you male chauvinist—"

"Don't say it, Leah, it's such a tired cliché."

"I'll say what I damn well please, cliché or not! What makes you think touching your hand means I'm ready to hop into bed with you?"

"You seem to have an overactive imagination," he answered, his deep voice hard.

"And it seems that a warm body is all you want from me!"

"You know better than that. Don't play games with me. I'm not a game-player."

"Neither am I. I just want things to be the way they were."

"No, I don't think you do. Besides, that's impossible. Don't you know what you do to me?" he muttered, his eyes holding hers with a tense glare. "I can't help it if we're attracted to each other, that we can't be just friends ever again."

"But I want us to be. I want—"

"You want me as much as I want you."

"No."

"Oh yes."

"Jace."

"Damn, it Leah," he growled, gripping her shoulders. "Admit—" His words halted abruptly and his hands dropped away as he heard Sue walking down the hall. But even when his sister came back into the room, his gaze remained locked with Leah's for several long moments.

"Dinner will be ready in a few minutes," Sue announced, coming walking through the door. She paused, sensing the tension in the room. Her voice faltered a bit as she added, "I hope you're both hungry."

"Starved. But excuse me for a few minutes, Sis," Jace said, his tone daunting as he stalked out of the living room. "I'll be back before you get it on the table."

Biting the edge of her lower lip, Leah closed her eyes briefly. She opened them again as she felt Sue staring at her back. With a weak smile, she turned to face her.

Sue eyed Leah speculatively, then planted her hands on her hips and asked, "Okay, what gives?"

Leah struggled to swallow. "It's nothing really."

"I don't believe that. I know my brother, and something's going on between the two of you. Do you want to tell me what it is?"

Leah shrugged. At that moment, she wasn't sure what she wanted.

CHAPTER FOUR

"It's—well, Jace and I are attracted to each other and that bothers me," Leah finally said, needing to discuss the problem with someone. "He's still married."

"He won't be much longer."

"I know he expects a divorce, but Erica could still come back."

"Ha! Don't kid yourself. He's through with her," Sue declared adamantly. "She was never right for him. That marriage was doomed from the beginning, although Jace tried a lot harder than she did to make a go of it."

"I know he did. I saw them together often enough to realize he was trying to be patient with her," Leah murmured. "But I know he believes marriages should last. Who's to say he wouldn't give her another chance if she decided to come back?"

"Jace knows his own mind. He wouldn't take her back, Leah. He lost all patience with her the day she left, and who can blame him? You know how she is, all smiles and charm at first, then after she gains your trust she uses you any way she can."

Leah smiled humorlessly. "I get the impression

you don't like her much."

"I did at first. She's one of those people who make a good first impression, but it's all downhill after that. The manipulator underneath starts showing through. No, I don't like her at all now. Do you?"

"No," Leah admitted. "I'd come to see through her too. When she left, she arranged things so I had to be the one to tell Jace she was gone, and that was before I knew he'd asked her to leave. I think she did it just to make me uncomfortable."

"Erica's happiest when she's making somebody squirm. Jace wasn't willing to put up with her nonsense, and since she could never make him dance to her tune, she was as ready as he was to split up. It's that simple, Leah. They're not going to reconcile. Jace had more than enough of her the first time around. And I can see why. During their last six months together, all she did was complain about having to live on this 'godforsaken ranch,' as she called it."

"I knew she was restless, but I had no idea she complained constantly. Jace never told me that. In fact, he rarely talks about her."

Sitting down on the edge of the chair, Sue shook her head. "Of course he doesn't. Jace is usually pretty open about his feelings but there are things he keeps hidden. He's not the kind of man to go around criticizing his ex-wife to anybody who'll listen."

"I'm not just anybody," Leah said softly, "I'm a friend. And since he seems to want me to be even more than that, it would help if he could confide in me."

"Give him a little more time to open up," Sue suggested. "Or are you still afraid to get involved with him?"

"I will be until the divorce is final."

"Afraid you might get hurt?"

"Yes, that's something I have to think about."

"I can't really blame you. I'd be cautious, too, if I were in your place. But what about after the divorce?"

"Well, I suppose things will be different then."

"It won't be much longer. And I have to tell you, you couldn't do any better than Jace."

Leah grinned. "You're prejudiced."

"True," Sue admitted, grinning back. "But he is a good man."

"I know," Leah murmured, gazing thoughtfully out the window. When Jace returned to the living room several moments later, she looked up at him. He glanced at her, his expression inscrutable. Emotion tugged at her heart. He was a wonderful man: witty, exciting, intelligent, sexy. And despite all her caution she was already involved. He just didn't know it yet.

More than a week later Jace got tired of waiting. He had held back from seeing Leah for three days after the divorce had become final, but now he wanted to see her too much to stay away any longer. He walked across the road, his hat shielding his eyes from the glare of the midafternoon sun. After knocking on Leah's kitchen door and getting no response, he looked around and finally spotted her unrolling wire fencing for the chicken coop. He started toward her as she hammered a staple into the wooden post to hold the wire in place.

"Afternoon," he said, coming up behind her.

She jumped and spun around. "Good Lord, Jace,

I didn't hear you coming! You must walk like a cat."

"I'm sorry. I didn't mean to startle you." Smiling apologetically, he surveyed her work. "You handle that hammer pretty well."

"I should. I got enough practice with it working on the house."

"You're doing a good job," he said, looping his fingers over the fence. "But why didn't you ask me to help you put it up?"

"I didn't want to bother you," was her soft answer as she dusted her hands off on her jeans. "Neighbors can get tiresome if they're always asking for something."

"But you're not always asking and I'm glad to help. Got another hammer?"

"In the toolbox over there. I'm nearly finished, though. You don't have to help."

"We can get it done faster working together."

He was right. They soon finished the chore, and Leah closed and latched the reinforced gate with a smile. "I'm glad that's done. My hens should be safe now. Oh, by the way, did Buddy give you my thanks for getting rid of the fox?"

"He gave me your message."

"I was so happy the trap worked and we didn't have to kill it."

'Let's just hope he hasn't found another henhouse to rob. His next victim probably won't be as tenderhearted as you."

"Maybe the time he spent in the trap helped him mend his ways."

"You've been watching too many Disney movies," Jace teased as he picked the toolbox up, laughing. "A reformed fox? I doubt it. But maybe he'll stay out of trouble. I told Buddy to let him go as far away from any houses as possible, somewhere he can find a pretty little vixen."

"Well if he does, I hope their children don't migrate back this way," Leah said. "I might not be as merciful with the next fox that goes after my chickens."

"I'll keep the trap handy just in case you need it again," he answered disbelievingly, his smile indulgent.

As they walked side by side to the house, Leah glanced at him. She was relieved to see he seemed far more relaxed than he had the night she had met Sue. It was good to feel at ease with him again instead of having to grapple with a distressing pall of tension. When they reached the screen door, she smiled at him. "How about a beer as payment for the work you did?"

"Deal." Removing his Stetson, he followed her into the kitchen.

"The toolbox goes in the broom closet over there," she said as she opened the refrigerator. Taking out a chilled bottle of beer, she opened it and poured the beer into a glass mug. "Here you go."

He raised one eyebrow. "Aren't you going to join me?"

"Sure, but iced tea would hit the spot better with me right now."

Taking a sip of beer and wiping the foam off his upper lip, he watched as she filled a tall glass with ice and poured the tea. He put his mug down and lightly clasped her upper arm when she started past to join him. "Leah, I have something to tell you."

Her hands began to tremble a little. Ice clinked in her glass as she gazed up at his tanned face. "Yes?"

"I'm not married now. I haven't been since Tuesday."

"Tuesday," she repeated, sheer joy making her heart skip a beat. "I knew it would be over soon, but I didn't know exactly when."

His darkening blue eyes held hers captive. "Are you going to tell me now that you wouldn't feel right getting involved with a divorced man?"

She shook her head. "No, I'm not going to tell you that."

"Does that mean I can kiss you again—finally?"

"That's what it means, Jace, yes," she whispered, closing her eyes as he bent his head down to her. She expected explosive passion, and was surprised when his lips chastely brushed her cheek. But it wasn't an unpleasant feeling. His touch had been gentle, seeming to indicate that it was more than a physical attraction that drew him to her. And of course she wanted much more than that. When he straightened, her gaze met his, and she felt they were beginning anew. She sat down happily at the table with him and took a sip of the minty tea. "Have you heard from Sue since she went back to Atlanta?"

"She called to let me know she got home safe and sound," Jace said. "Other than that I haven't heard from her, but I'll probably get a letter some time next week. She says I'm too slow writing back, but we keep in touch regularly."

Leah nodded. "That's good. I like her very much."

"She likes you, too. Said she enjoyed her visit here

that Wednesday."

"I'd only been teasing when I said I'd put her to work, but she insisted. I appreciated the help."

"She really didn't mind," Jace said. He took another swallow of beer, his gaze never leaving Leah's face. "Have any plans for the rest of the day?"

"Nothing exciting. I hoped to get the upstairs hall and one of the bedrooms painted. I've already put the drop cloths down."

"I'm a top-notch painter. Want me to lend a hand?"

"Like Sue's, that's an offer I can't refuse. Painting isn't one of my favorite chores, but it won't be so boring if I have you to talk to."

"See?" he said, humor lighting his eyes. "I'm a good man to have around."

"You're the best neighbor I have."

"I'm the only neighbor you have."

"True. That might have something to do with it," she teased, laughing when he playfully tugged a strand of her hair in retaliation.

Three hours later, Leah stood in the doorway of her bedroom, admiring the clean ivory walls in both her room and the hall. "It's really an improvement over that faded robin's-egg blue, don't you think? And the lighter color makes my room look larger. I like it."

"Me too," Jace agreed, replacing the lid on a paint can. "Where do you want to store this?"

"In the shed. We can clean the rollers and brushes out there too," she answered. Picking up the two pans they had used, she led the way down the stairs and outside to the shed.

"Good thing we used latex paint," Jace murmured after they had finished washing everything, taking a crisp white handkerchief out of his pocket. Wetting a corner, he cupped Leah's jaw in one hand and gently washed her cheeks. "You got a few splatters, but they're coming off."

"Thank you," she said softly, excited by his closeness and tender touch.

"You have beautiful skin."

"And freckles."

"Just a few. Here," he said, running his fingertip along the ridge of her nose. "I think they're cute."

"Mom tried to convince me of that when I was about fifteen and doing everything I could think of to get rid of them."

"And now?"

"Now I'm not fifteen anymore and they don't bother me."

"Good, because I like them."

"I'm glad you do," she said, smiling up at him. "But I never expected to be standing in a shed discussing my freckles with you."

Laughing, he finished washing her face. "There, the paint's all gone. You look as fresh as a daisy."

"I feel like a wilted one. Ready for another beer?"

He nodded and followed her back into the house, where they were met by strong paint fumes. "You probably won't be able to sleep in your room tonight," he said. "I doubt the place will be aired out enough by then."

"The paint fumes do usually give me a headache. I'll probably move into one of the other bedrooms."

"That won't help much. The fumes are all over the house. Maybe you should stay at my place."

She eyed him with some suspicion despite his

bland tone, but had to grin in return when he grinned.

"No strings attached," he added, pouring the cold beer she handed him. "I'm just trying to be neighborly."

"To tell the truth, I don't want to wake up with a headache in the morning, but ..."

"I promise I won't barge into your room in the middle of the night and have my way with you. Unless, of course, you insist."

She had to laugh. "Still ..."

"You'll be perfectly safe. I'm a gentleman. Trust me."

She did trust him. But could she trust herself? Of course she could, she decided. Leah knew how to say no even when her body wanted her to say yes. Even a man as magnetic as Jace couldn't seduce her unless she was willing to be seduced. Finally, she nodded. "Okay, I accept your kind invitation."

"Good, but I'm afraid you'll have to take potluck for dinner."

"Let me take care of dinner. Do you like omelettes? I have plenty of fresh eggs."

"Sounds great. In fact, all this talk about food is making me hungry." Finishing the last of his beer, he stood. "Why don't you get your stuff, and then we can go."

"I want to have a bath first. Then I'll come over. All right?"

Nodding, he picked up his hat and left.

With the omelettes, they had salad and white wine. It was a light but satisfying meal made all the more pleasant by interesting conversation that ranged from politics to movies.

"I didn't know you were a movie buff," Leah said while they cleared the table. They carried their plates into the kitchen and stacked them in the dishwasher. "What are some of your favorites?"

"Oh, I have several. And now that I can get them on videotape, I've started a collection," he told her, smiling softly as her eyes lighted up. "Would you like to watch one tonight?"

"I'd love to."

"Then let's go into the den and you can pick the one you want to see."

"Oh, this is great," Leah commented moments later as she scanned the cassettes lining a bookcase. "You already have so many to choose from I don't know which one to pick."

"Most of the recent films are on the bottom shelf."

"Oh, I see." She bent down, then shook her head. "I think I'd rather see one of the old classics, if that's okay with you."

"Fine. I like them all. Which will it be?"

She looked over the selection again, then eagerly plucked one out. "*Dark Victory*. I haven't seen it on the late show in years."

Jace cocked his head to one side. "You're sure? It has a sad ending. Bette Davis dies, remember?"

"Ah yes, but she does it so dramatically."

Grinning, he took the cassette from her and put it in the machine. "We can't start it yet, though. Have to make popcorn. A movie's not a movie without it."

"Want me to help you?"

"I can handle it."

While he was in the kitchen, she continued to survey the film collection. It was quite varied. There were comedies, dramas, adventures, a couple of westerns, and even a few cartoon features. When Jace returned to the den a short time later, she said over her shoulder, "It must be wonderful having all this entertainment right at your fingertips. I may have to think about buying one of these, though machines and I usually don't mix. I think they hate me. I bought a small computer for the studio and it tried to give me a nervous breakdown. Everything went wrong with it."

"Videocassette players are fairly simple. You shouldn't have any trouble with one."

She turned around as he put the bowl of fluffy popcorn, the bottle of wine, and two glasses on the low table in front of the brown leather sofa. "Hmm, I've never had wine with popcorn before."

"If you'd rather have a soda or—"

"No, this is fine. This is the perfect way to spend an evening—watching a great old movie in a cozy den."

"This is the kind of evening Erica detested," Jace said flatly.

Smoothing the skirt of her green cotton dress self-consciously, Leah sat down on the sofa, wondering if he would say more.

He didn't. Not about Erica anyway. He pushed all thoughts of her out of his mind. Their relationship—or rather the lack of a very meaningful one—had been a major disappointment for him, and he refused to let bad memories ruin a pleasurable time with Leah. He switched off the lights and started the movie.

Leah was soon caught up in the story. Although she had seen this original *Dark Victory* several times and knew what to expect from beginning to end, the movie was still able to ensnare her in its emotional grip. She and Jace watched the tragic story unfold in silence, emptying the bowl of popcorn and sipping wine. When the final, heart-wrenching scene faded and the credits rolled, he waited a couple of minutes before turning on the table lamp next to him. He looked at Leah, unsurprised by what he saw.

"I knew you'd cry," he whispered. He pulled out his handkerchief to dry the crystal rivulets of tears that trickled down her cheeks. "I knew you couldn't watch this movie and not cry."

She smiled tremulously. "Your eyes aren't completely dry either."

"Nonsense. Must be your imagination."

"No. You're not as tough as you look, Mr. Austin."

"Oh, do I look tough?"

"Most ranchers do—or they're supposed to. You know, lean and hard as nails."

"And that's how I look, huh?"

"Sometimes. But that's on the outside. On the inside I do believe you have a soft heart."

"How can you be so sure?"

"I just know. A woman can tell," she murmured, tentative fingertips touching his sun-browned face, her warm green eyes beckoning him.

He silently pulled her into his arms, covering her mouth with his.

Neither Jace nor Leah could deny the hunger they felt. Their lips met and parted repeatedly, then their kiss deepened, and their tongues met in an arousing, erotic dance. Leah had never felt so totally alive and attuned to the spirit of any man. Jace was different from any she had ever known; he was much more important to her. She cared about him deeply and wanted to give all of herself to him without reservation. She had never felt that way before, and it was a heady experience. She couldn't possibly attribute the dizziness she felt to the wine she'd had. It was Jace himself who was intoxicating, the feel of his skin, the faint scent of his woodsy after-shave, his tenderly marauding kisses.

"Sweet. You're so sweet," he whispered gruffly. His arm around her waist pulled her closer and he felt her body relax softly against his. Her mouth tasted like honey and ambrosia, an aphrodisiac that fanned the fires of desire in him, making him ache to know her completely. Winding the silken swathe of her hair around one hand, he tilted her head back to trace circles of searching kisses over the slender column of her neck.

"Yes," she gasped, trembling when he nibbled her earlobe with his teeth. His warm breath tickled her and set off a chain reaction that ignited the nerve endings of every inch of her skin, overwhelming her with licking flames of passion. As Jace moved the heels of his hands up and around the straining sides of her breasts, she unfastened the buttons of his white shirt and trailed her fingers over his broad chest, her nails catching in the fine dark hair. Her lips curved into a woman's secret smile against his as he shuddered slightly, as much in her power as she was in his.

Slowly, ever so slowly, he lowered the zipper at the back of her dress and dropped the scoop-necked bodice down around her waist. Turning her so she was lying across his thighs, he released her lips to gaze down at the rapid rise and fall of her breasts. The darker circles of her nipples were visible through the transparent fabric of her bra and he rubbed his fingertips over them, hearing the soft catch in her breath. With one hand, he deftly unfastened the hooks and eased the straps off her shoulders, removing the sheer garment completely. His own breathing became shallower, faster. Her beautiful breasts seemed to be inviting his touch, but he made her wait for that first, longed-for contact.

Leah's eyes fluttered open and encountered the smoldering blue coals in the depths of his. Transfixed, she couldn't look away from him, and their searching gazes held moment after sensual moment.

Excitement heightened the color in her cheeks and her tender lips parted.

"You're so lovely," he murmured. "I have to touch you, kiss you." Unable to wait any longer, he drew one hand through the deep valley between her breasts, then spanned one peak with his thumb and forefinger. "Here. And here. Yes, Leah?"

"*Yes*," she whispered, tingling all over as he began to trace delicate circles around one breast to the rosy summit, before treating the other to the same lazy caress. Her eyes half closed, she watched his tan hands upon her ivory flesh and her limbs weakened in the wake of the waves of delight that swept through her. Needing to be closer to him, she pressed nearer, trapping his large yet sensitive hands between them. Her arms tightened around his shoulders as her lips brushed over his and she boldly tantalized the tip of his tongue with her own.

Moaning with pleasure, he eased her back on the

sofa cushions and bent over her, his lips following the dry trail his fingers had blazed upon her rounded flesh. He felt her tense suddenly when he closed his mouth around one tip, then she relaxed and cupped his neck in her hands. In the lamplight her skin shimmered, and he kissed every soft, resilient inch of her breasts, his tongue inscribing erotic patterns and teasing her succulent nipples.

With his mouth he gave exquisite pleasure, and an aching emptiness bloomed centrally within her. His firm male flesh invited her own caresses and she feathered her fingers over his strong back, exploring the structure of his spine with a light touch. Then her nails toyed with his flat nipples until a tremor rippled through him and his lips claimed hers with a plundering demand.

She held him tight and kissed him back as his hands ranged over her, molding every curve and contour. Then he slipped his hand beneath the hem of her dress and drew it up between her bare thighs. When his fingers started to glide under the elastic band of her panties she stiffened. This time she couldn't relax again. She wanted him. Yes, she wanted him more than she'd ever wanted anything in her life. Her body clamored for the satisfaction only he could give. Yet in the corner of her mind misgivings still lingered. He was becoming so important to her. She liked him, perhaps too much, and that meant she could be hurt by him. She simply wasn't ready to make such a complete commitment. Reaching down, she stilled his hand.

Groaning against her mouth, Jace raised his head slightly and looked down at her. "Too soon?"

"Yes. Oh Jace, I know it seems I'm always saying no to you. And tonight . . . I shouldn't have let things go so far but I—it all happened so fast. I just can't. It *is* too soon."

He sat up and silently rubbed his face with his hands.

She touched his right forearm, but pulled her fingers away when she felt the tensing of his muscles. "Besides," she added weakly, hoping to ease the tension, "what if Buddy or one of the hands walked in on us?"

"You don't have to worry about that. It's Saturday night and they've all gone into town for a big time." Jace looked back down at her, a tight, rather sardonic smile appearing on his lips when she covered her breasts. He sighed. "Leah, I don't want to rush you but I have to be truthful. I don't know if I can take any more episodes like this. It isn't that easy for a man to turn off desire."

"It isn't easy for a woman, either."

"You just did a nice job of it."

"That doesn't mean it was easy. You swept me off my feet and I had to fight to come to my senses."

"Tell me, Leah, what can I do to persuade you to give up the fight? It's inevitable. You know we're going to be lovers," he said quietly.

She had no answer to that and her eyes held his until he dragged his gaze away and rose from the sofa.

"You better get dressed," he said, starting across the room. "I'll be back in a few minutes."

Sitting up, she pulled her dress around her as he strode toward the door. "Where are you going?"

"To take a cold shower. I need one."

He glanced back at her, his expression warm and understanding. Then he was gone. Leah knew that if she hadn't already fallen in love with him, she was very close to it.

CHAPTER FIVE

The following Friday afternoon, Leah went into the Carousel Boutique, next door to her studio. The little bell above the door jingled merrily and Marlene Decker, the owner, looked up from the display of evening purses she was arranging.

"Howdy, stranger," she sang out with a wide smile. "Taking a break from work?"

"No appointments this afternoon. I should be in the darkroom right now, but I'm the boss, so what the heck?" Leah said lightheartedly with an airy wave of her hand. "I can't be fired for shirking my duties for a few minutes, and I want to look through your dresses. I'm going to splurge and buy one, even though your prices are outrageous."

"That's because I sell only the best clothes," Marlene retorted, combing her fingers through her coal-black hair. "What are you splurging for? Must be a special occasion."

"A night on the town. I want something more elegant and sophisticated than I have at home in my closet."

Marlene winked knowingly. "Ah-ha, it's for that

man of yours, isn't it? He sure has been keeping you busy this week. I've hardly seen you."

"Of course you have. We had lunch together Tuesday and Wednesday."

"But you usually take in a movie with Joe and me or have dinner with us at least one evening a week. This week you've deserted us. Of course, I can't blame you. I got a nice long look at your Jace Wednesday when he stopped by the studio. At least I think it was him. Tall and dark? Tiny little half dimples in his cheeks when he smiles?"

"Sounds like him, and he did come by Wednesday."

"You told me he might. That's why I was watching for him."

Leah laughed. "You're impossible."

"So my Joe says. But I'm not really. I'm just interested in the men in my friends' lives." Marlene gave a cheeky grin. "So how's it going with Jace? Getting serious?"

"Very serious, as far as I'm concerned," Leah admitted. "I'm in love with him."

Her friend clutched comically at her heart, feigning shock. "My Lord, I never thought I'd live to see the day you'd say you were in love. I've introduced you to at least a dozen men in the past year and you've never been the least bit interested in any of them."

"None of them was Jace. Don't get me wrong, they were all very nice, but Jace is something else again. For me, anyway. He's ... well, you know I've always liked and respected him. He's a warm, interesting person, and now that we're getting to know each other better I realize what a dynamic man he is. He's so endearing, so real, so—"

"All right, all right, I get the picture. How you do run on, just like a woman in love," Marlene teased. "Still," she added, "you need to remember that no man is perfect."

"I didn't say he was."

"You were coming mighty close. Is he getting serious too?"

"I hope so. Like you said, he has been keeping me busy all week. I do know he cares about me."

"There's no chance that his ex-wife might come back and mess everything up, is there?"

"No chance at all. Jace has told me a little more about his marriage in the last couple of days, and although he hasn't said it in so many words, I get the distinct impression Erica gave him hell—or tried her best to. I think he's kind of angry at himself for ever marrying her in the first place."

Marlene nodded thoughtfully. "Doesn't sound like he's pining for her to come back to him."

"Hardly."

"Then there's nothing standing in your way."

"Except maybe my own caution. But that's beginning to dissolve."

"A sexy man you're in love with will do that to you every time."

"Yes. Fun, isn't it?" Leah replied. "Now, about that dress."

"Look through these, I just got them in," Marlene said, leading her to the small alcove. "You're sure to find something you like, something that'll knock his socks off. I'll be back with you in a minute. The lady browsing in sportswear can't seem to make up her mind. I'd better go help her."

Leah went through the dresses in her size. A few were outlandish, but most were designed along classic lines. After much consideration, she chose a black chiffon dress with spaghetti straps and a shirred skirt that swirled prettily around her knees when she turned.

Marlene agreed with her choice. "It's perfect with your hair and that light golden tan."

"I love it. But I'll have to hem it."

"Free alterations, remember? Babs," Marlene called to her seamstress in the back room. "She'll pin it up and have it ready for you in a couple of hours."

"She doesn't have to rush. I don't need it until tomorrow. Tonight Jace and I are just going to watch a couple of movies at his place."

"Ah, that sounds cozy and romantic."

"It is." Leah answered with a bright smile and a happy heart.

Jace arrived at Leah's the next night carrying a large bouquet of wild bluebonnets, which he presented with a flourish. "Picked just for you."

"They're beautiful. Thank you," she said, touching one delicate blossom as she stepped back to let him in. "Let me put them in water and I'll be ready to go."

"You look great in that dress," he remarked, his gaze wandering over her as she filled a vase with water. "Is it new?"

"Yes."

"I like it."

"Thanks." Turning, she surveyed his gray suit.

"You look very handsome tonight."

He frowned. "Just tonight?"

"Oh, I didn't mean it to sound like that. I—"

"I'm only teasing," he replied with a slow grin. "I know what you meant, and thank you for the compliment, ma'am."

"You're more than welcome, sir," she returned blithely as she finished arranging the heavy clusters of bluebonnets. "Well, I'm ready to go if you are."

"We'd better. I made the reservation for eight."

They drove into Dallas to the Chanterelle. It was a fine restaurant with an intimate atmosphere and dancing, and it had been wise of Jace to make a reservation. Couples without one were being turned away with apologies when Leah and Jace arrived. The maitre d' showed them to a table in a quiet corner and a waiter materialized almost immediately to ask if they wanted anything to drink. Both of them decided on white wine. Leah sipped it slowly a few minutes later as she looked over the menu.

"I think I'll have the lobster," she said at last. "And their specialty salad. I had it once and it was delicious."

"You've been here before?"

"A couple of times. I like it. I'm glad we came."

"I thought you might enjoy dancing after dinner," Jace said, looking over the gold-bordered menu one last time before closing it. "I'll have the lobster too. It'll be a nice change."

Leah looked at him with raised eyebrows. "Did I hear a hint of resignation in your voice? Is Cookie still giving you fellows steak and potatoes every night?"

"At least four times a week. I've warned him the

hands are liable to quit if he doesn't start giving them a little more variety."

She shook her head. "They won't quit. They like working for you too much."

Jace looked at her inquiringly. "Who told you that?"

"Buddy. He said most of your hands have been with you for a long time and wouldn't think of going to work anywhere else. And Buddy's been at the ranch how long? Twenty-five years?"

"Almost. Dad hired him when I was just a kid, so he's like one of the family. Sue adores him."

"He really loves both of you, too."

Jace gave her a rather odd look. "Buddy told you all that?"

"Shouldn't he have?"

"It's not that he shouldn't have, I'm just surprised he did. He's not much of a talker. How did you get him to open up?"

She batted her eyelashes and drawled coquettishly, "I'm just naturally charming, I guess."

"Yes," Jace agreed softly, his hand covering hers on the tabletop, his thumb playing with her fingertips. "You are that."

She'd only been joking but he was serious, and his words heightened the happiness she invariably felt when she was with him.

Over dinner they talked and laughed. In their secluded corner, Leah was scarcely aware of the other people in the restaurant, except for the waiter. He checked on them periodically, and when they'd finished their lobster he came to ask if they would like dessert.

She shook her head. "No, thank you."

"You should try our raspberry torte," the waiter persisted. "It's delicious. The Chanterelle is famous for it."

"I know. I've heard about it. I shouldn't though," she said without much conviction as she met Jace's knowing eyes. "But I'm going to. It sounds too good to pass up."

"I'll have it too," Jace told the pleased waiter, who left quickly before she could change her mind.

Leah wrapped a tendril of hair around one finger and sighed. "I really shouldn't do this."

"You don't have to watch your figure, I'm watching it for you."

"Oh, that joke's as old as the hills," she responded. She cast her eyes heavenward, but was unable to suppress her laughter.

He laughed with her. "Okay, it was bad, but I'm not a comedian."

"I noticed."

Still smiling, Jace touched her shining hair. In the candlelight, it shone like spun gold and felt like the finest silk between his fingers. His gaze held hers and there seemed to be no need for words as they simply looked at each other for several precious moments.

After dessert, Jace lit a cigarette and leaned back in his chair.

Leah tilted her head to one side. "I thought you were going to quit."

"I'm trying. Making progress too. I'm only smoking a few a day now."

"How many's a few?"

I don't know. Five or six."

"That's not too bad, but none would be better."

"Worried about my health, Leah?"

"Aren't you?"

"Don't be coy."

"Me?" Suppressing a smile, she pressed her hand against her chest and shook her head. "I wouldn't even know how to be coy."

"All women know how, at least a little," he replied, crushing the cigarette out in the ashtray. He reached for her hand. "May I have this dance, Miss—" He halted abruptly as a man stepped up to the table.

"Johnny, how are you?" Leah's smile was welcoming. "I didn't know you were here."

"I didn't see you either until just now on my way out," Johnny said, glancing at Jace. "Just wanted to say hi."

Leah introduced the two men. "Jace Austin, Johnny Enders."

Standing, Jace shook Enders's hand. "Care to join us for coffee?"

Johnny glanced back at Leah. "If you're sure I wouldn't be intruding."

"Of course not. Take that chair behind you and I'll try to get the waiter's attention," Jace insisted cordially, though he wasn't really thrilled with the newcomer's timing or with the way he was looking at Leah. But his mother had raised a son with manners, so he beckoned the waiter as Johnny Enders sat down.

"Well, Leah, I didn't expect to see you here," Johnny said, smoothing his blond hair. "I haven't been back since the time we had dinner here together. Do you come often?"

"No. Tonight's the first time I've been back too."

"Quite a coincidence."

Quite, Jace thought. But it was a coincidence. He had chosen the Chanterelle for dinner; Leah had never even mentioned the restaurant to him.

"Marlene told me you finally had dinner with Joe and her the other night," Leah was saying. "She really enjoyed it. Says she sees much more of me than she does you."

"Well, you know Marlene. She'd like me to call her every day and tell her exactly what I'm doing," Johnny joked. "And naturally she sees more of you with your studio right next door to her shop. That's a super dress, by the way. Did you buy it from her?"

"Yes. Whenever business is slow, I go buy something from her and she comes over to have her picture taken. Makes us feel more productive and less worried about going bankrupt."

"Nonsense! Not in that location. It's the most profitable business district in Fort Worth."

"I know. That's why you advised Marlene to open her shop there. I was just kidding about the bankruptcy," Leah assured him. "Johnny is a city development consultant," she explained to Jace.

"Houston alone must keep you busy, considering its rate of growth," Jace commented, resting his chin on steepled fingers. "Must be an interesting job."

"I think so. Actually, I travel all over the States, wherever my firm sends me. And what are you in, Jace?"

"Cattle ranching."

"Oh? Where?"

"My place is about twenty-five miles north of Fort Worth."

Johnny snapped his fingers. "You're close to Leah then?"

"Just across the road."

"Of course. I've seen your place. Looks like a nice spread. How big is it?"

"Medium-size. Big enough to keep me busy."

"Well, this has been great, but I have an appointment, so I'd better run along now," Johnny said, taking a swallow of his coffee before rising. Then he bent down to give Leah a brief kiss on the cheek. "Great seeing you. I'll call you sometime. Jace, hope to run into you again."

"Pleasure meeting you, John," Jace answered. He watched as Enders dashed away, buttoning the coat of his tan suit. "Seems like a nice fellow."

"He is." Leah smiled. "He's always on the go."

"So he's the one you came here with?"

"Once."

Jace's eyes narrowed as he regarded her intently. "Where did you meet him?"

"His sister, Marlene, owns the boutique next to the studio. She introduced us."

"Go out with him often?"

"A few times."

"And?"

"And I like him. He's a good friend," Leah murmured, smiling faintly. "What is this? An inquisition?"

"I'm just curious."

"Now your curiosity's satisfied. Weren't you about to ask me to dance before Johnny happened along, Mr. Austin?" she prompted. "If the offer still holds, I accept."

"It still holds," he said, reaching for her hand to

lead her onto the dance floor.

She went into his arms, keeping her smile to herself. It warmed her through and through to realize that Jace was interested in the other men she knew.

The music was slow with a sensuous beat, and they moved together in perfect rhythm. After a while, they simply swayed to the romantic tempo, his arms around her waist, hers across his shoulders, her forehead resting against his neck. Her very warmth aroused him and the clean fresh scent of her hair mingling with the light fragrance of her perfume made Jace hold her tighter still. Against his large frame, she felt delicate, almost fragile, but every inch a mature woman. He wanted to push the straps of her dress aside and cover her shoulders with kisses, but this was neither the place nor the time.

Leah relaxed in his embrace, her eyes closed. The hardness of his long, lean body fascinated her and she wished she could dance forever with him this way. It was good to be so close to him, to feel his muscular arms around her and his warm breath stirring wisps of her hair. Yet deep within she needed more, and perhaps he sensed it. When she nuzzled her face against his neck, he pulled back to hold her a short distance from him. When she looked up at him their gazes locked.

He had to kiss her. On the romantically lit dance floor, she was totally irresistible. Her shimmering hair framed her beautiful face, and her full bow-shaped lips enticed him. Jace leaned down to sample their sweetness, and passion shot through him like an electric current as she ardently responded.

"Leah, let's get out of here," he gently suggested,

leading her back to the table. After taking care of the check he handed her her purse and they left.

Outside, while they waited for the parking attendant to bring Jace's car around, he drew Leah into the shadow of an evergreen shrub to kiss her again. And again.

"We'd better stop. Now," she finally breathed, hands curving over his upper arms. "If we keep this up much longer, we might get arrested."

A low chuckle rumbled in his throat as he reluctantly led her to the curb. He helped her into the car, tipped the attendant, and pulled away from the restaurant.

On the way home Jace held her hand securely, pressing it down on his right thigh until at last he lifted it to his lips and kissed her fingers, each in its turn. Her palm stroked his jaw. His slow smile curved against her skin as he murmured, "We could pull off the road somewhere and neck."

In the soft glow of the dashboard lights, she smiled back at him. "I don't think that's a good idea. I'd rather not have a highway patrolman shine a flashlight in our faces and say, 'Okay, move along now, kids.' If we're going to neck, we'd be better off doing it at my place."

He nibbled the tip of her index finger. "Is that an invitation?"

"I don't know," she whispered, her pulse thundering in her temples as she saw the passionate intent flare up in his eyes. "I—I guess it is."

One by one, he kissed her fingertips again.

When they arrived at her house, he opened the passenger door for her and she stepped out of the car.

Leah's heart seemed to skip every third or fourth beat.

She lifted her face to the star-studded sky and inhaled appreciatively. "The air's so fresh here. And the moon's so bright. Look at it."

He did, then followed its magical beams back to her. She was enchanting. He slipped an arm around her narrow waist to direct her toward the house. "Let's go in."

Once inside her cheery kitchen, Leah experienced a fleeting moment of residual caution and pulled away from him. "Would you like a drink? Or coffee? Anything?"

"Only you," he answered unevenly, putting his arm around her and leading her into the parlor, where he switched on a table lamp. His gaze swept over her, hot and intense, then he touched her face, her hair, her neck. "Leah, I want you so much I'm not sure I can let you go again."

A sweet thrill coursed through her and she released her breath in a tremulous rush. She wanted him too. Accepting that irrevocable fact, she cupped his jaw in her hands. "Kiss me, Jace."

He did, his warm firm lips devouring hers. He felt her tremble, tightened his arms about her, and lowered her onto the sofa behind them. She pressed against him, her lush lips opening like a flower to his. He tasted the sweet nectar of her mouth, his tongue making a brief but tantalizing foray within.

Leah unknotted his tie, slipped it from beneath his collar, and unfastened the top button of his shirt. Lowering her head, she kissed the base of his throat as his hands cupped the sides of her breasts for a moment before straying lower, to her waist and the gentle curve of her hips. She felt gloriously alive, attuned to his every caress. Never before had she experienced such a wondrous sense of closeness with anyone. Jace was so special and it seemed in that moment that her love for him doubled and redoubled, overflowing in her heart.

With a light breeze whispering through the trees outside, they held each other in the cool room, losing themselves in long kisses. Her lips clung to his as her fingers slid under his shirt to stroke his strong shoulders. She loved the smooth firm texture of his skin.

"I can't keep my hands off you," he whispered as they coursed like fire over her. He sought the scampering pulse in her throat and flicked the tip of his tongue over it, making it beat faster. "You feel so good, taste so good. I can't get enough of you."

Several lovely minutes later, he held her away from him long enough to shrug out of his coat. Then he pressed her hands against his shirtfront. "Unbutton it for me, Leah. Take it off."

She did so with enticing slowness, unfastening his cuffs at last, then pushing the shirt from his shoulders to draw it down inch by inch while she laced kisses across his chest.

"Woman, you're driving me crazy," he playfully growled, pulling his arms free of the sleeves to span her waist with his hands. "Now it's time for me to do the same to you."

Her heart fluttered with excitement as he swiftly unzipped and removed her dress. He tossed it aside and it floated to the floor in a whisper of chiffon while his boldly roving eyes took in her loveliness. The soft swell of her breasts rose above the cups of her strapless black bra and a long side slit in her matching half-slip exposed the length of her shapely thigh. He trailed his fingers over it, down to her knee and back up again, wishing away even the sheer barrier of her pantyhose between her skin and his. His gaze met hers momentarily before he closed his mouth over the peak of her right breast. A luscious morsel of flesh rose erectly, straining the dampened fabric of her bra, and he gently tugged at it with his teeth.

"Oh, Jace," she moaned softly, unable to find the words that would express how she felt.

"Honey, you still have too many clothes on," he murmured. Unfastening the back hooks, he lazily peeled the diaphanous cups away and exposed her breasts to his impassioned gaze.

She felt as if his eyes were igniting fires beneath the surface of her skin. Then he touched her, and intense heat consumed her, body and soul. "Jace," she urged, covering his hands with her own, pressing them harder against her rounded flesh. His lean fingers etching circles on her sent a series of delightful shivers down her spine. She caressed his naked chest and back.

He looked down at her, reading the desire in her emerald-green eyes. "You are beautiful, Leah."

"You make me feel like I am."

"You are, believe me."

"So are you, Jace." His answering smile was so tender that there was a little catch in her heart as she curled a hand over the nape of his neck and drew his head down. "Kiss me some more."

"I may never quit."

And she hoped he wouldn't, as their lips brushed together, parted, brushed again, teasing, tasting, exploring. His arm supporting her bare back lifted her tighter against him as her sweet breath mingled with his.

Leah trembled when his mouth sought her breasts, his lips and teeth and tongue rousing her desire and his own to a fever pitch.

"I *need* you, Leah. I want us to do the most pleasurable things together."

"Jace..."

"Honey, please don't say no this time."

"I—I don't want to say no," she confessed, leaning back in his embrace to gaze up at him. She had to express her honest feelings. "But this isn't a casual thing for me."

"It isn't casual for me either."

"I want us to make love because you mean so much to me. I really care about you, Jace."

"I care about you too, Leah. Surely you know that."

"I...hoped."

"Well, I do care about you. Very much," he said seriously, his eyes darkening.

She believed him, and her joy seemed endless. With a tremulous smile, she outlined the finely chiseled shape of his lips with a finger until he caught its tip between his teeth and gently nibbled. He trailed feathering kisses over her wrist and up her inner arm to the slope of her shoulder, and she held him close.

"Your skin's so soft," he whispered into her ear. "I have to see all of you, Leah. Let's go upstairs."

"I . . . precautions. I mean, I'm not prepared for this."

"I am."

She pulled back to look at him. "You were awfully sure of yourself. Or me."

He shook his head. "I wasn't sure at all. I just didn't want you to have any excuse to say no again."

"Do you always plan ahead to the finest detail?"

"Whenever I can. Especially when I want something. And I've never wanted anything or anybody as much as I want you right now. Come to bed, Leah."

"Yes," she said, wanting him too, wanting him enough to relax when he swept her up in his arms and carried her upstairs to her room. He put her down to stand by the bed, switched on the lamp, then turned back toward her. She'd never known a moment as thrilling.

"You still have too much on," he murmured. "Undress for me."

Inhaling deeply, she stepped out of her shoes but went no farther as her gaze beckoned him. "I think I'd like you to undress me this first time."

"My pleasure." He moved nearer and reached out to lower her half-slip to the floor. He removed her pantyhose, then her panties more slowly, and then he took both her hands in his and raised her arms out slightly to the side. Faint, enchanting color rose in her cheeks as his smoky blue eyes traveled over her. He pulled her to him. "Don't be shy with me, honey."

"I'm not shy really," she answered, aware of the proof of his aroused masculinity against her abdomen.

"It's just that you have me at a disadvantage. You still have clothes on."

"We can remedy that situation in a hurry," he quipped. He stripped quickly, kicking off his shoes and undoing the buckle of his belt. "Now, it's all fair."

His skin was like burnished copper and he was as magnificent as he had felt to her touch through his clothes. His broad chest tapered to lean hips, and his legs were long and powerful. Leah caressed his hair roughened chest until he leaned away from her to toss the covers down to the foot of the bed. Anticipation made her gasp softly when he abruptly swung her up and lowered her onto the mattress, lying down with her, propped up on his elbows.

He cradled her face in his hands. "It feels like I've waited forever for this."

"I know," she sighed. And she did. Now, loving, feeling loved, she was ready to give herself as she had never given before. Jace was the one she had been waiting for and it was right to be with him this way. Deep in her heart, she knew it and felt a growing joy. She touched his chin, repeating, "I know."

"Now the waiting's over. God, if you only knew how much I need you."

"I think I do, Jace, because I need you too."

"Show me," he challenged, his slow smile teasing but his tone serious. "I want to know how much."

"This much." Her parted lips found his. "And this." Her mouth opened wider. "And this." She sought the tip of his tongue with her own.

"Temptress," he said gruffly, his responsive kiss demanding and hungry. "Seductress."

"Oh no, not me." Her lips curved beneath his.

"You're seducing me—that's why I've resisted so long. I always knew you'd be able to, sooner or later."

"Mmm, and now that I've finally succeeded, you're at my mercy," he said, a deliberate inflection of theatrical villainy in his melodious voice. "You're mine to do with as I please."

"Oh, sir, such words make me feel faint," she pretended to protest, giggling until their eyes met and his low laughter ceased. She swallowed hard.

"You are mine," he reiterated, his voice dropping, intent.

She was his, wanted to be. Eagerness bubbled up in her and she kissed his temples, his chin, the faint indentations in his cheeks that always deepened when he smiled. "You smell nice," she whispered, inhaling the subtle scent of his after-shave. "So nice, Jace."

"God, so do you. Like flowers in spring." He buried his face in her hair, then spread it out in a golden fan on the pillow. He ran his fingers through its silken warmth, looking down into eyes that never wavered from his. Her eyes were beautiful, a deep green flecked with golden desire. He kissed them shut, feeling the tickling fringe of her lashes flutter against his lips. "My sweet Leah."

His words, his kisses, everything he did, weakened her limbs. The feel of his lean body against her inflamed her senses. She wrapped her arms around him, delighting in his masterful caresses as she caressed him too. Their tongues played over each other, around each other in an erotic ballet as their mouths merged together with compelling heat.

"I have to taste. Everywhere," he promised, beginning with her warm uptilted breasts. He plied first one and then the other with lingering kisses. Her silken flesh radiated an irresistible heat that seemed to intensify in the roseate peaks. These he took in his mouth each in turn, drawing each deeper inside, with slowly graduating pressure. He felt the tremor that rippled over her and her small hands floated down his back and then up again, her nails lightly skittering along his spine.

Together, they created a realm all their own. The rest of the world ceased to exist, and nothing mattered but the two of them and their growing knowledge of each other.

She learned how coaxing and persuasive he could be.

He learned how ardently responsive she was.

Holding him, caressing him, she realized he loved to feel her fingers run through his hair.

He found that the entire expanse of her back was sensitive to light stroking touches.

It was a time of discovery, and they both were enslaved by the pure pleasure of it. Time had no meaning. A soft breeze drifted in the window and across the bed, caressing their skin, but doing nothing to cool the wealth of warmth they shared.

"Touch me," Jace commanded softly, guiding her hands down, pleased when her slender fingers curved around him. "Yes."

Leah sighed with delight when he moved his lips over her breasts, her midriff, her abdomen. His tongue encircled her navel. He kissed her long legs, the soles of her feet, even the tips of her toes.

"Tickles."

"Mmm."

"Jace," she whispered when he parted her legs and grazed his mouth along her inner thighs. His warm breath swept upward and felt exquisite. He slowly trailed his hand down from her waist toward the very center of her femininity, and when he touched her there at last, she quivered with pleasure.

He explored her tenderly, his fingertips charting the hills and secret valleys, driving her wild as piercing sensations quickened. Eyes half closed, she watched his hand play between her thighs and felt almost faint in the rush of emotional and physical bliss he elicited.

He looked at her face. Her lips were parted. Her eyes glimmered and there was a sensual glow overlying her delicate features. He groaned softly as she continued her caresses and his need for her rose to a nearly intolerable level.

"Jace," she gasped as he ran his fingers lightly over her again. "Love me, Jace."

"Oh, I'm going to," he said huskily, lowering himself onto her. He cradled the back of her head in his hands. "I'm not going to let you go all night."

She glanced at the lamp. "The light . . ."

"Leave it on. I want to keep looking at you."

"Oh Jace, love me now."

"Relax, honey," he coaxed, feeling her tense instinctively when he pressed against her. "I'm going to be very gentle with you, I promise."

"I . . . know you will," she murmured. His hard body throbbed against her and she covered his taut buttocks with her hands, urging him closer. "Now."

"Oh, Leah." Thrusting tenderly, he entered a velvet sheath of warmth that slowly blossomed open to welcome him. Her breath mingled with his as his lips captured hers.

She pressed her nails into his lower back when he thrust deeper, then again until he filled her completely, uniting with her, making them one. Lost in the tingling awareness of partial fulfillment, she swept her fingers through his hair, more in love than she had ever imagined she could be. He scattered kisses across her forehead and temples.

"Okay?" he asked, his tone hushed.

"Wonderful," she answered, gazing up at him when he raised his head. She saw the warm glint of triumph that flashed briefly in his eyes and the tiny smile of understanding that graced his firm lips. His affection for her was clearly visible. She couldn't look away from his beloved face. Even when he began to move within her and she matched his rhythm, her gaze held his.

"You're a delight," he told her.

"And you're a very sexy man, Mr. Austin."

"Say that again."

"You're sexy," she gladly obeyed. "Irresistible. You make me forget all my inhibitions."

"Oh honey, I hope so," he muttered, still moving in a gentle rhythm.

He was patient, a generously giving yet gloriously demanding lover. With deliberate finesse he gained the responses he wanted. His every kiss and caress, every movement of his virile body conveyed an insistent message which she answered with growing abandon. She eagerly learned the lessons of lovemaking he taught, discovering what pleased him and herself as well. Probing the delicate shell of her ear with his tongue, Jace whispered intimate words and she found herself saying things she had never thought she would want to say to any man, even him.

He knew he would never forget the faint fragrance of perfume that clung to her smooth skin or the feel of her arms and legs around him. She was exquisite in every way. It was all he could do to hold his own passion in check as he sought to satisfy her.

"I might not ever let you go," he warned hoarsely, nuzzling her jaw. "Ever."

"Never stop," she breathed, trembling. "I don't want you to let me go."

"*Honey.*"

"Oh—" Her fingers dug feverishly into his muscular shoulders as he slipped one hand beneath her and lifted her higher, delving deeper still. He created a rippling of flutters that radiated outward from her very core, and with every second that passed those flutters quickened and became more keen.

Together, they spun upward, ever upward, transcending level after level of sensation, each one more imperative. The flutters became a continuous tide crashing through her, never ebbing, forever heightening.

"Jace," she softly cried out, clinging to him. "Take me."

He had to. Moving faster, harder, he immersed himself in her, the heat in his loins swelling, setting him on fire.

Then she flew up to the ultimate spire, moaning as she was suspended on the fine edge and wrapping herself around him, urging him to join her there.

He had no choice. He had wanted to make it last longer but he wanted her too much. "Leah," he growled, no longer capable of gentleness as he found release in her sweet, throbbing flesh. Together, both breathless, they drifted back into downy-soft fulfillment.

Some minutes later, Leah stirred lazily in Jace's light embrace. Beneath her hand that rested upon his chest she could feel his heartbeat slowing, returning to its normal rate as her own was. She felt fantastic, and her love for him had strengthened, entwining her soul in links of fine chain from which she never wanted to be released. She sighed dreamily.

"What's that sigh mean?" Jace gently inquired, his lips touching her tousled hair. "Sorry it happened?"

She shook her head. "I'm not sorry at all. You?"

"You must be kidding!"

She laughed and wriggled closer against him, nestling her cheek in the hollow of his right shoulder. "Ah, Jace, you're really a nice man."

He smiled to himself. "And you're a very good lover, Miss Bancroft."

"You're not so bad yourself, Mr. Austin."

"Is that all you can say, 'not so bad'?"

"You want more?"

He chuckled. "Only if it's the truth."

"Okay, the truth is you're a wonderful lover," she murmured. "And I'm glad I allowed myself to find that out."

"Oh, so am I. I'm not sure I could have waited much longer for a night like this with you."

"Sex maniac," she teasingly accused, running her fingertips over his chest. "That's what you are."

"Where you're concerned, I guess I am," he conceded, drawing her closer against him. "And this is just the beginning."

"Promise?"

"Yes."

"Mmm, that's what I wanted to hear," she whispered, smiling faintly as he tightened his hold on her. Feeling perfectly content and very much in love, she drifted off to sleep.

CHAPTER SIX

Leah answered the phone in her studio after the first ring, and wished she hadn't. "Hello, Erica," she said. "How are you?"

"Fine. Busy, busy, busy. Life in Vegas is nonstop, you know," Erica proclaimed. "I love it."

"That's good."

"Oh yes, I'm much happier than I was on that godforsaken ranch. I called Jace last night but he wasn't in a very talkative mood. That's why I'm calling you. How's he doing?"

Leah took a deep breath. She was hardly eager to discuss Jace with his ex-wife. In fact, that was the last thing in the world she wanted to do, so she answered as noncommittally as possible. "He seems fine."

"Think he misses me?'

Leah's hand tightened around the receiver. "I don't know, Erica. I suggest you ask him that."

"Ha! He wouldn't admit it if he did."

"Why do you want to know if he misses you? Do you miss him?"

"You know, I do, a little. After all, we did have our good times, especially at first. So what's Jace been up to since I left?"

Leah bit back an impatient sigh. "I don't know why you're asking me all these questions. Why don't you ask Jace?"

"I tried but he can be so tight-lipped. When I called him last night he just wouldn't talk. I thought you could tell me how he is."

"As I said, he seems fine. Busy running the ranch, as usual."

"Yes, that damn ranch," Erica replied sharply. She paused a second, then said more lightly, "And what have you been doing with yourself since I escaped from the back country? Still making family portraits and taking care of your chickens?"

"That's about it," Leah answered flatly. "Listen, Erica, I really can't talk now. I have to set up for my next appointment. But I'm glad to know you're happy in Vegas."

"It's an exciting place. Ever been?"

"No. Maybe someday. Erica, I really have to get to work."

There was a long silence at the other end of the line. Then Erica spoke again, her voice hard. "You don't like me much, do you, Leah?"

"I don't dislike you. But I have to tell you that I don't appreciate the note you left for Jace when you went away," Leah stated plainly. "You knew I didn't want to tell him you'd left him, especially when you led me to believe he had no idea you were going. You forgot to mention the fact that he'd asked you to leave. Telling him to go to my house in your note was a crummy thing to do."

"It seemed so impersonal to tell him I was gone

in writing. I thought it would be better if you told him."

"No you didn't, Erica. I think you just wanted to humiliate him and embarrass me. You like to do that. It seems like making other people feel bad makes you feel important somehow."

"Oh dear, Jace has been telling you some ugly things about me."

"No he hasn't. He rarely talks about you, in fact. And I didn't need him to tell me how you enjoy manipulating people. I was beginning to realize that before you went to Vegas."

"You're really not being fair," Erica protested, her voice purring again. "I don't try to manipulate people."

"Yes you do. You're trying to manipulate me right now. You can deny it forever but that doesn't change the way you act. It took me a while to see through you, but now I do. Sorry, but that's just how I feel."

"You're wrong."

"No, just not as gullible as you obviously think. And I really do have to hang up now."

Erica gave her no chance. The phone in Vegas was slammed down in Leah's ear, and she replaced her own receiver with a grimace of distaste.

Later that afternoon, Leah walked out of her darkroom just as Marlene entered the studio. "Can't stay long," her friend announced as she flopped down into a chair. "Just came over for a little chat."

"Good. Maybe that'll take my mind off my troubles."

"What's wrong?"

"Nothing really. I'm just a little out of sorts," Leah

said, dropping down on the settee. "Erica called me after lunch."

"What did she want?"

"To know if Jace misses her."

"Terrific. What did you tell her?"

"To ask him."

"Why does she want to know anyway?"

Leah shrugged. "I'm not sure. She did admit she misses him a little."

"And what does that mean?" Marlene questioned. "Do you think she wants him back? Oh Leah, try not to worry. After all, you told me he wouldn't have her."

"I don't think he would. But if she came waltzing back into his life, she could make things uncomfortable. She's good at doing that."

"From what you've told me about him, he'd send her packing soon enough if she tried any of her shenanigans."

Leah's face brightened. "You do have a point there. And I do know he wouldn't put up with her nonsense. It's just that I wish she hadn't called."

"I presume you didn't tell her about you and Jace?"

"No. If he wants to, he can. As far as I'm concerned it's none of her business."

"There you are, then. Forget about her," Marlene advised. "Let's change the subject."

Leah was happy to.

That evening at her house, over dinner, Leah smoothed her napkin over her lap as she looked across the table at Jace. "I had an unexpected phone call today," she said. "From Erica."

He frowned, his eyes narrowing. "What did she have to say?"

"Not much. She asked about you. She said she called you last night but you didn't talk much."

"That's true. I was nice to her, but I think we've said about all there is to say to each other. She asked you about me? What was it she wanted to know?"

"If you seem to miss her."

Jace regarded Leah somberly. "And how did you answer that?"

"I told her she should ask you."

"And if she did ask me, what do you think I'd say?"

Leah spread her hands. "I'm not sure. She was your wife, so I guess it would be normal for you to miss having her around once in a while."

"Wrong," he proclaimed, setting down his glass to reach across the table for her hand. "I don't miss her, even once in a while. The marriage was a mistake, and to be honest it's a relief not to have her in the house. I don't miss her at all, Leah."

"Okay," she murmured, nodding understandingly. He wasn't lying either to her or to himself. Sure of that, she breathed a silent sigh of relief, feeling better than she had since the phone call.

Leah was happy. For nearly three weeks, she and Jace had spent every night together except two, when he had flown to Houston on business. It wasn't simply their lovemaking that made her feel so good; it was their entire relationship, which continued to grow and expand. Every day, she felt closer to him. It was as if they were made for each other. They shared so many interests and could talk about anything together, or they could be comfortably silent. It was even more exciting to wake up every morning. Being in love was more fantastic than she had ever dreamed possible.

One evening she was humming in the shower when she thought she heard Jace coming up the stairs. She listened to his footsteps in the hall and smiled when he knocked once and opened the bathroom door.

"I'm back," he announced. "Buddy just wanted to talk about buying a couple more horses. You almost finished?"

"Just got in here."

Grinning, he pulled the shower curtain open. His gaze rambled over her from her toes to the top of her head. "Mmm, you look very nice all wet."

"As I recall, you always look nice wet, too," she murmured, reaching over to drape her arms around his neck. "I think you should join me."

"You do?"

"Yes." She moved sinuously against him. "Come on. Take a shower with me."

"How can I refuse an invitation like that?"

"I hope you won't."

"Not a chance," he said, smiling wickedly at her as he began stripping off the clothes she had already made damp.

The moment he finished undressing, he stepped into the tub and drew the curtain shut. He backed Leah against the tiles, planting his palms against the wall on either side of her head. A devilish sparkle appeared in his eyes. "Now, my dear, you're trapped. You can't get away from me."

Laughter bubbled up in her. "You really are fun, Jace."

"You ain't seen nothing yet, lady." He grasped her waist, lightly tickling her ribs until he allowed his hands to journey upward to her breasts.

Her giggling ceased as his fingers massaged and caressed. Her blood rushed hotter through her veins as she reached for the bar of soap, which she rubbed over his shoulders and chest.

"Keep touching me like that and I might forget we're supposed to take a shower first," she cautioned. "Turn around please." She lathered his back, moving the soap in slow circles down his long legs, over his calves to his ankles and feet, then back up again over his shins and knees.

"Ah, this is the life," he murmured, watching her smooth the creamy foam over his midriff. "I wonder if harem girls do this for their masters."

"Maybe so, but I'm not a harem girl. We live in a modern world," she retorted, her smile teasing as she plopped the cake of soap into his hand. "In other words, you scratch my back and I'll scratch yours. It's my turn now."

"Come here then," he commanded, starting with her shoulders and working down her back to her waist and her firm, rounded bottom. His arms encircled her, then his hands drifted up across her abdomen to her breasts. With long, lingering strokes, he covered her firm flesh with bubbly foam, then moved his fingertips over and around the rising slopes, sketching evocative designs in the frothy layer of soap that clung to her skin. His thumbs brushed over her nipples again and again. Fascinated by the instantly aroused tips, he toyed with them.

She reveled in his touch, in his closeness, in the

love she felt. Her gaze glided over his bronzed body, so overtly masculine and spellbinding. She looked up at him. Their eyes met. He kissed her, his warm lips opening her mouth.

"Jace," she breathed. "You're driving me crazy."

"I know. But like you said, it's your turn now and I've just started."

As he bent down to lather her shapely legs, she touched his dark hair, which was covered with a fine mist. He eased a hand upward between her thighs to caress her knowingly, exploring her secret contours and making her ache for him. She swayed slightly, feeling dizzy with desire. His intimate touch was much too brief, but the brevity of it made it no less electrifying. When he drew her with him beneath the fine spray to rinse off, her every nerve ending was tingling and seemed to literally catch fire as he followed a trickle of water that ran over the swell of her breast, licking it away. She wrapped her arms around him, her eager kiss seeking his.

He swept his hands over her, arching her against him. Need consumed him and he stepped over the side of the tub and helped her out. Taking two towels off the shelf behind him, he dried her as she dried him, both of them taking their time about it, enjoying each other. But at last he could wait no longer. "I'm taking you to bed."

'Hurry," she urged, her emerald eyes aglow with rising passion. "Oh hurry, Jace."

Lifting her up in his arms, he carried her out of the bath and down the hall to her room.

"Leah," he muttered, easing her down onto the mattress. When he joined her he pulled her on top of him, and hands spanning her waist, he raised her high, his mouth wandering over the sweet roundness of her breasts. She settled down upon him, rotating her hips slowly, enveloping him in her inner warmth. He arched his hips upward, driving deeper within her.

"Oh Jace!" she softly exclaimed. "I love you so much."

"I love you," he groaned, lost in the pleasure she freely gave.

Considerably later, after they had tumbled down together from piercing ecstasy to supreme fulfillment, he held her in the crook of his right arm, smiling sleepily as she moved her hand over his chest. His eyes started to close.

"I photographed the sweetest baby today," she said suddenly, rousing him inadvertently from his doze. "She's ten months old and that's really a nice age. She was adorable, so cuddly and friendly, smiling at the drop of a hat. Such a doll. I almost wanted to bring her home with me. Of course, I've never seen a baby yet that I could resist. Do you like babies, Jace?"

"I guess I do," was his quiet answer. "I haven't been around that many."

"They're so sweet. I think I'd like to have two or three some day. What about you?"

He said nothing for a moment. Then he murmured, "I'd like to have children, sure. But I'm in no hurry. There's plenty of time."

"That's true," Leah mumbled, unsuccessfully trying to stifle a yawn as she settled herself closer to him. "But you should have seen that little girl today.

She was such a sweetheart."

Within minutes Leah was asleep. But Jace was now wide awake. Moving carefully, not wanting to disturb her, he reached for the pack of cigarettes on the bedside table and pulled one out. He lit it and stared solemnly through the darkness at the glowing tip. Memories of Erica raced through his head, nearly every one of them unpleasant. He moved his fingers lightly over Leah's waist. He cared about her, probably loved her, yet he wasn't sure. After all, he had once thought he loved Erica but it turned out he hadn't. Would his feelings for Leah die the same quick death? Or hers for him? He didn't know. All he knew was that he wasn't ready to make another commitment yet just to see it come to nothing before his very eyes. But he hated the thought of telling Leah that, although he knew he had to. It was the only fair thing to do, but that realization didn't make him feel any better about it.

"You're very quiet today," Leah said to Jace after breakfast the next morning. "Something on your mind?"

"Yes, something we have to talk about," he answered, looking her straight in the eye. "Leah, I think we should stop seeing each other for a while."

The words were so unexpected they didn't sink in for a moment. "Are you kidding?" she murmured. The somber expression mantling his features told her otherwise and she felt as if someone had delivered a hard blow to her stomach. "No, I—I can see you're not joking. But why, Jace? Why should we stop seeing each other?"

"I guess I should have said that differently. Of course we'll see each other. I meant I think we'd better cool it for a while."

"Why?"

"Because I'm not ready to get involved again," he replied frankly, his tone gentle. "My experience with Erica taught me not to rush into another commitment, Leah. I need to back off a little."

Leah stared at him, feeling physically ill. Heat washed over her, followed by an icy chill, then heat again. She shook her head. "But Jace, I'm not Erica."

"I know you're not. You're nothing like her, thank God."

"And you've known me longer than you knew her before you two got married."

"Right now, I know you better than I ever knew her," he conceded, his face rather drawn as he lit a cigarette. "But I still don't want to rush into anything until I'm sure it can work out. I don't want another failed marriage."

"Marriage?" Leah repeated weakly. "I never even mentioned marriage to you."

"No, but if we go on this way, you might start thinking about it."

"I might. I probably would... someday."

"And when you started talking about children last night, I—"

"Is that what's bothering you?" she exclaimed softly, her expression incredulous. "Good heavens, Jace, I just made an innocent comment about the baby I photographed yesterday, because she was such a doll."

"And you asked me if I want children."

"Well, the subject had never come up before, and I was curious," she replied, a trace of impatience edging her voice. "Just because I asked you a simple question doesn't mean I'm eager to get pregnant."

"Someday, you'll want marriage and a family though, won't you?"

"Sure, I guess I—"

"I don't know if I can give you that, Leah."

"Have I ever asked you to?" she snapped, defensive anger mingling with intense disappointment. "I really don't know what you're so worried about."

"Us. Where we're headed. The mistake we might make if we're not careful. I don't want to get married again until I'm sure it'll last."

"I don't know if any couple's ever sure. The best they can do is expect it to last, hope it will, and work hard at it. There are very few guarantees in life."

"Let me try to explain exactly how I feel," Jace said quietly, his eyes troubled as they scanned her face. "My parents had a wonderful marriage. They were devoted to each other and so happy and content together. I expected my marriage to be the same. But Erica and I . . . well, needless to say, I was very disillusioned about our relationship. I don't want to go through that again—that's why I need some time to think about us, time alone."

Leah was devastated. The burning ache of tears that needed to be shed gathered behind her eyes and a faint pain began throbbing in her temples. She couldn't believe what he was saying, didn't want to believe it. As close as they had become— as she'd thought they'd become—he was ending it. A dull heaviness settled in a hard knot in her chest as she simply looked at him.

"You said you love me."

Anguish crossed his face. "God, Leah, I think I do love you, but—"

"You think? Well, isn't that just dandy?" she shot back, the pain she felt surfacing in resentment. "Is that supposed to make me feel better?"

"No. This isn't easy for either of us. But please try to understand why I'm doing this."

"Oh, I understand perfectly."

"I don't think you do. Leah, I care about you," he declared earnestly, starting to lay his hand upon hers on the tabletop and sighing when she jerked it away. "I think I am in love with you. That scares the hell out of me."

"Don't insult my intelligence by handing me that line," she said, lifting her chin. Unable to sit still any longer, she stormed across the kitchen and started furiously polishing the counter with a dish towel. "That's the oldest excuse in the book for giving somebody the brush-off."

"This time it happens to be the truth, and it's not a brush-off."

"Then what would you call it?"

"Time-out. I just need time to think."

She clutched the towel tighter. "Fine then. Take the rest of your life to think, if that's what you want, Jace. But don't expect me to wait here and hold my breath while you decide."

He stood and started toward her, but stopped in the center of the room when she raised a halting hand. Feeling lousy, he raked his fingers through his hair. "Leah, if you'd just try to understand why—"

"I understand just one thing. I was reluctant to get involved with you in the first place, but you convinced me I could trust you. I told you our relationship was much more than casual for me. You said it was for you, too. Silly me, I believed you," she muttered, glowering at him, determined to hold the tears back. "I've never been so involved with any man as I was with you—you must know that without a shadow of doubt. That's what I understand. You let me think you were as serious as I was but you were really just having a little fling."

"That's not true, Leah. Believe me—"

"I've done too much of that already. How gullible do you think I am?" she replied stiffly, managing to keep her lips from trembling. "If you don't want us to see each other anymore, fine. I'm certainly not going to beg you to change your mind."

"I'd never expect you to and it's certainly not what I want," he muttered, his jaw tensing. "You're being a little unreasonable about this, Leah."

She could gladly have slapped him for that, but ignored him instead.

"You're upset. I am too," he added. "We'll talk about this later."

"I think we've said all there is to say." She inclined her head toward the back door. "I want you to leave now. I have to get ready to go to the studio."

"Leah, a little understanding on your part would help a lot. I'm sorry. This—"

"Just go."

Muttering a curse beneath his breath, Jace picked up his Stetson, slapped it against his right thigh, and walked out.

When he was gone, she made a small noise in her throat that caught in a sob, and flung the damp dish towel at the door he had closed behind him. It made a faint wet spot on the wood and slid to the floor in a heap. The suppressed tears rushed forth in a torrent then, cascading down her cheeks and she bent over the counter burying her face in her folded arms.

CHAPTER SEVEN

Jace started pacing back and forth across his front porch about two o'clock Saturday afternoon. Leah hadn't come home Friday night and he was concerned, anxious. Every time he heard a car approaching he hoped it would be hers, and when it wasn't, his frown deepened a little more. Squinting, he stared across the road at her house, wondering where the devil she could be. Even if she had decided to stay in Fort Worth last night, why wasn't she home yet? She kept the studio open only a half day on Saturday, closing at twelve, so she should have been home by now. He'd called the studio around eleven and left a message on her answering machine. That wasn't unusual; she often used the machine to avoid interruptions while she was photographing. The problem this time was that she hadn't returned his call as he had requested. Although he knew she was upset with him, he didn't think she'd simply ignore his message.

Worry darkened his eyes. Maybe she had fallen and hit her head in the darkroom and was lying there unconscious ... if she had even gone to the studio today. What if she'd had an accident on the way home last night? What if . . . ? What if . . . ? The possibilities that came to mind were highly disturbing and his face was grim as he thrust his hands into his pockets. He heard another car coming, and waited for it anxiously but when it came into sight it wasn't Leah's, and he gritted his teeth impatiently. He could no longer stand around doing nothing. Turning, he strode purposely to his study.

First he phoned the highway patrol. No accident involving a Leah Bancroft had been reported. He contacted the hospitals in Forth Worth and Dallas next and was told each time that no one by that name had been admitted. Relief surged through him as he hung up after calling the final hospital, but it was relief that didn't last long. He still didn't know where she was and it wasn't like her to just go off without telling him. Before, whenever she'd gone to see her parents on holidays or occasional weekends, she'd asked Jace to care for her chickens and look after her place. The very fact that she hadn't done so this time made him feel something must be wrong. He supposed she could have left the chickens enough feed for a few days, but deep in his heart, he doubted that was the case. She was genuinely fond of the cackly hens and the strutting rooster. If she was going to be away she wanted someone to look in on them. But . . .

Thoughtfully rubbing his jaw, Jace stared at the collection of movie cassettes without actually seeing them. Suddenly, he snapped his fingers. Leah's parents! Even if she wasn't visiting them they would probably know where she was. He'd call them. Remembering she had mentioned her father's name was

Zeb, he dialed directory assistance in Austin, but was informed that no Zeb Bancroft was listed.

"Any Bancroft with Z as the first initial?" he inquired hopefully.

"No sir, nothing at all with a Z," the male operator said politely. "I do have a Zebulon in the unlisted numbers, but of course I can't give it to you."

"I understand. Thanks anyway," Jace murmured, and replaced the receiver in its cradle.

"Damn it," he swore softly, glancing at his wristwatch. It was nearly three o'clock. Bounding out of his chair, he returned to the porch to scan Leah's driveway, which was still ominously empty. Striking a closed fist on the wood railing, he decided to go to her studio. Maybe she was working late and had been too busy to check her answering machine. He had to find out if she was there or not.

Taking his keys from his pocket, he started toward his car, but stopped suddenly when he saw Cookie amble out of the bunkhouse and stare up at the bright blue sky. Perhaps, just perhaps, Leah had come home late last night and left again very early this morning. Jace wondered if maybe he'd simply missed seeing her. If he had, Cookie probably hadn't. He got up earlier than anybody else to get breakfast for the hands.

"Hey, Cookie," Jace called, walking with long strides across the dusty ground to the older man, who greeted him with a nod. "Did you happen to see Leah's car in her driveway when you got up this morning?"

Cookie pondered. "Let me see now. Nope, don't reckon I did. 'Course, I don't recollect looking over thataway. Might've been there. Might not."

"Okay, thanks." Jace started to turn away, but turned back again. "Why didn't you go into town with the rest of the boys? It's Saturday."

"Don't I know it?" the cook drawled, a smile etching his weathered features. "Ain't never missed a Saturday night in town yet. Don't plan on missing this fun, neither. The boys took the truck. I'm going in the Jeep. Wasn't ready to go when they were—had some business to attend to."

He didn't elaborate and Jace certainly didn't press him. Long ago, he had learned Cookie didn't care for personal questions, and he respected that. With a sketchy salute he started back toward the car. "See you later."

"Jace," Cookie sang out, giving him a crooked grin when he turned around once more. "Want me to fix you up a steak before I take off?"

"Thanks, but no thanks," Jace answered wryly, opening the door of the Volvo. "Matter of fact, I'm going to Fort Worth to buy you a recipe book so you can feed us something else once in a while."

Cookie chuckled, appreciating the joke. "Since you're gonna be in town, have a drink with us. You know where to find us."

"Maybe I will," replied Jace as he folded himself into the driver's seat. "I'll see." But as he drove away from the ranch, his smile quickly vanished. He just hoped he'd find Leah at the studio, perfectly safe. Risking a speeding ticket, he reached Fort Worth in record time, but he didn't find Leah. After pounding on the studio door loudly enough for her to have heard him in the darkroom and receiving no response, he went next door to the boutique. He knew

Leah was friends with the owner, Marlene. But Marlene wasn't in. Wouldn't be back until Monday, the young saleswoman in the shop told him, discreetly admiring the lines of his long trim body.

"Do you know Leah Bancroft?" he inquired. "The photographer next door."

"Oh sure, I know Leah."

He shifted his weight from one foot to the other. "I've been trying to get in touch with her without any luck. Do you think she might still be in the studio? I knocked, but maybe she didn't hear me."

"Oh, she's gone. Matter of fact, I saw her lock up."

"What time?"

"Um, let me see. About twelve thirty, I think."

"Do you know where she was going?"

"Home, I guess," the clerk answered, eyeing him curiously. "I don't really know. Why are you asking? Is something wrong?"

"I hope not," he muttered, heading for the door. "Thanks for your help."

"But I didn't help."

"You did a little." And she had. Now at least he knew Leah had been in the studio that morning. That eased his mind to some extent, but not a great deal. He still had no idea where she was at the moment. Why the devil hadn't she gone home?

Turning that unanswerable question over and over in his head, Jace started his car, shifted into gear, and pulled away from the curb. He didn't know where to look for her, which made him feel helpless—not a pleasant experience. His hands tightened around the steering wheel, his knuckles whitening with the pressure he applied. He swung to the right at the next intersection, hoping a drink with the hands would do him some good.

The Round Up was a modest little restaurant where the food was simple and invariably delicious. But Jace had no appetite, not even when fragrant aromas greeted him as he walked in the door. Buddy spied him immediately and waved him over to the roughhewn oak table that most of the ranch hands were sharing.

"Grab yourself a chair," he invited Jace. "Been a long time since you came here on a Saturday night. What'll you have, Jace?"

"Beer, please," Jace told the waitress who appeared as if by magic at his elbow. She returned in less than a minute and he took a slow sip as the country band tuned up. He was hardly aware of Buddy, Cookie, and the rest of the hands as they called out hello to people they knew and flirted with the women. Some of the hands found dance partners and swung them out onto the floor, while the others tapped their toes in time with the music. Jace couldn't relax. He decided to go back to the ranch—maybe Leah would be home by now. Leaving a nearly full glass of beer, he rose to his feet. "See you fellows tomorrow."

"Wonder what's gnawing at him?" he heard Cookie ask as he dropped money onto the table and walked away.

"I don't know," Buddy replied, "but he sure does seem to be riled up about something."

Riled wasn't the right word. Jace was worried.

Leah was miserable. She had intended to enjoy the

jazz concert, but found herself paying little attention to the talented musicians and singers. Shifting restlessly in her seat, she felt Johnny Enders's gaze boring into her and turned her head to give him a wan smile.

"You're not enjoying this, I can tell," he whispered, taking hold of her elbow. "Let's go."

She didn't protest. He was right. She wasn't having a good time, although she had meant to try her best to. She couldn't keep her mind off Jace and the pain he'd caused her. Wondering if he was happy tonight with his precious freedom and lack of involvement, she walked silently with Johnny across the parking lot to his sleek red Maserati.

"Do you want me to take you back to Marlene's?" he asked after they got in. "Or would you like to stop someplace for a drink?"

"It's still early," she said. "And I wouldn't mind a brandy."

"Terrific." He started the engine. "There's a nice tavern a couple of blocks down the street."

The tavern was nice, the atmosphere quiet and relaxing. They slipped into a corner booth and ordered their drinks. Johnny leaned across the table, his hands folded together as he looked at Leah. "Aren't you feeling well?"

"I'm fine."

"You're not. Something's wrong."

"I guess it is kind of obvious, isn't it?" She smiled apologetically. "When I called and asked if you wanted to go to the concert, I planned to be lively and vivacious all evening. It didn't work out that way. I'm sorry, Johnny."

"Hey, don't worry about that. I'm just sorry something's bothering you. Like to talk about it?"

There was a slight downward curve to her lips as she shrugged. "I don't think so."

"Might help if you did. Does it have anything to do with your rancher friend, Jace Austin?"

"I didn't realize I was so transparent. Or maybe it's always easy to tell when someone's lovesick."

"So you are in love with him. I got that impression when I saw you together at the Chanterelle," Johnny said. "What's the trouble? Isn't he in love with you?"

"That's the crazy thing. He says he thinks he is," Leah murmured, smiling at the waitress who set her brandy and Johnny's bourbon down on the table. "Jace got a divorce recently. His marriage was short but far from sweet. He says that's why he's shying away from another commitment."

"But you don't believe what he says?"

"I don't know." She shrugged again. "It's pretty hard to believe him. I mean, it seemed easy for him to end what we had together."

Johnny jabbed a piece of ice with the swizzle stick. "He's making a big mistake, giving you up."

Leah smiled. "Are you just trying to make me feel better, or do you really mean that?"

"You know I mean it." Johnny smiled back. "You know you could have avoided all this with Jace if you'd gotten involved with me instead. But you decided we should just be friends."

"And you are a good friend," she said simply. '"Nice enough to let me cry on your shoulder like I'm doing now. Any time I can return the favor, let me know."

Nodding, Johnny took a sip of his drink. "I hope I won't be needing your shoulder, though. No serious involvements for me. I'm playing the field."

"And there's not even one woman who's more special than the others?"

"Not yet. I've decided I might be a lifelong bachelor."

"I doubt that. One of these days you'll fall head over heels. Remember to invite me to the wedding when it happens."

"What makes you so sure it will?"

"Because you're not the type to be a loner."

Johnny lifted an eyebrow. "Meaning you think maybe Jace is?"

"I don't quite know what to think about him," she admitted huskily, watching the brandy swirl in her glass as she twirled the stem between her fingers. "I can't figure him out."

"What are you going to do about him?"

"There's nothing I can do."

"It must be hard living so close to him."

"I don't know yet. I haven't seen him since yesterday, when he told me he thought we should cool it. But I guess it will be uncomfortable, knowing he's right across the road."

"Thought about moving?"

Leah's head shot up, and determination glimmered in her eyes. "Not on your life! I love my place and I'm not about to give it up, Jace or no Jace. Besides, I'll get over him."

"I'm sure you will."

"Are you?" she asked hopefully. "Sure, I mean?"

"You don't sound very certain now."

"I guess I'm not really. I just have to keep telling myself I am."

Reaching over, Johnny patted her hand. "It will just take some time."

"I know." She took a deep breath. "Oh hell, enough of this. Let's talk about something else."

"Okay. Do you think the Astros have a chance of winning the pennant this year?"

She laughed aloud. "You know I don't keep up with baseball until the World Series starts."

"I know," Johnny acknowledged with a grin. "I just wanted to hear you laugh. You will keep your chin up, won't you?"

"You better believe it." The promise was for herself as much as him.

When Leah arrived home Sunday night, Jace saw her headlights as she pulled into the driveway. He left his house and walked across the road, his face a grim mask, reaching her as she was unlocking the side door. He grasped her elbow.

She cried out and spun around, able only to distinguish the shape of a man in the velvet darkness.

"It's me," Jace said curtly.

"Dear God!" she muttered, releasing her breath in a rush. "What's the matter with you? You can't just come out of the dark and grab somebody. What do you want?"

He didn't answer as she turned the key and opened the door. She stepped into the kitchen, flipping on the light, and he didn't wait for an invitation to join her. Sweeping up the suitcase she'd left on the porch, he walked in behind her and set the canvas bag on the floor. He straightened, and stood with arms crossed over his chest and feet wide apart, meeting the hostile look she gave him without a word.

The mere sight of him made her tremble inside with a mixture of emotions. But fear wasn't one of them no matter how he glared at her, and she refused to let him get even a glimpse of everything else she felt at that moment. Dropping her purse onto the countertop, she held her head high. "If you don't mind, it's late."

"It's very late," he growled, taking a half-menacing step closer. "Where the hell have you been?"

As if he had the right to know! Flags of angry color unfurled in her cheeks, though she managed to keep her voice cold as she said, "Ask that question nicely and I might answer it."

His left hand shot out to clamp around her right wrist. "Don't play games with me," he muttered through clenched teeth, a muscle twitching in his jaw. "I'm not in the mood for them."

"And I'm not in the mood to be manhandled. Let me go!"

"Not until you tell me where you've been all weekend."

As his grip tightened, she struggled to free herself, but the attempt was useless. He wasn't rough with her, merely unrelenting, and for her his touch was both agony and ecstasy. Because he could make her feel both, she experienced a brief but quite intense longing to pummel his chest with her fists. But that would have been far too revealing a response, not to mention too primitive. She successfully suppressed the urge to do him bodily harm and realized he didn't intend to release her. "Fort Worth," she said brusquely. "I spent the weekend in town."

"Without telling me you were going to. For God's sake, Leah, I didn't know what had happened to you!"

"Well now you know where I was." She stared at his hand. "So would you please let go of me?"

"Not just yet," he said, his eyes glinting like shards of aqua ice. "How could you go off that way without telling anybody you'd be gone all weekend?"

"I didn't. I asked Buddy to take care of the chickens while I was gone."

"Buddy didn't tell me that."

She raised her shoulders in a careless shrug. "Probably because you didn't ask him."

"How the devil was I supposed to know he knew? You've always asked me to feed the chickens before. Why didn't you this time?"

"Why Jace, I should think the answer to that is obvious," she drawled, inwardly pleased that he was upset. "After all, you're the one who wanted us to stop seeing each other. I certainly couldn't come asking you for a favor."

"Don't be ridiculous. I didn't mean it like that. Of course I want us to see each other sometimes."

"Oh. Then I must have misunderstood."

"I doubt that." He suddenly eased his grip around her wrist. "Why didn't you come home, Leah? Was it because you were upset about—"

"I had some shopping to do," she cut in, her face bland, hiding the truth. "And there was a jazz concert I wanted to attend Saturday night. I had plenty to do."

"Where did you stay?"

"With Marlene and her husband."

"And did they go to the concert with you?"

"As a matter of fact, they didn't. Joe doesn't care for jazz."

"You went alone then?"

"I didn't say that."

Jace's finely hewn features hardened. "Who did you go with then?"

"Johnny. Johnny Enders. I introduced you to him at the Chanterelle, remember?"

"Yeah, I remember. What I'd like to know is how he knew you'd be free Saturday night to go with him."

"He didn't. Actually, I called him and suggested the concert," Leah replied, her voice taking on an edge. "Not that this is any of your business, Jace. You want us to be neighbors, that's all. Fine. But good neighbors aren't busybodies. You tend to your business and I'll tend to mine."

Abruptly, he released her wrist. "If that's the way you want it."

"That's the way you want it," she corrected, striving hard to keep the proverbial stiff upper lip. "I told you I took our relationship seriously, and you pretended you did too."

"I did. Still do. Leah," he murmured, starting to brush the back of his hand over her cheek, the corners of his mouth pulling down in distress when she stepped back to avoid the caress. "I . . . You're very important to me. But I'm afraid you'll soon want more than I can give. When all this started between us, I didn't have any idea my experience with Erica could affect what we had together, but—"

"It has," Leah finished for him, her heart beating dully, her emotions stripped raw, although she wanted to conceal that fact. "Okay. Then that's it. We're neighbors again, nothing more."

"It'll always be more than that. We'll never simply be neighbors again."

"We'll have to try, I guess."

"Leah . . ." He shook his head, searching for the right words to explain to her what he was feeling. He had lost her trust. He hated that and wanted to regain at least some of it. Yet he doubted he could make her understand. She had never been married, never felt the disillusion that came creeping in when the marriage was a mistake. She had never known bitter episodes like he had experienced with Erica, those episodes that made him so cautious now. At a loss for words, he turned away and went to the door.

"I better go. You must be tired," he said softly. "'Night, Leah."

Her voice choked up on her, leaving her speechless. He went out across the porch, opened the screen door, and disappeared into the night. Alone in the kitchen with only the ticking of the wall clock for company, Leah allowed her previously straight shoulders to droop slightly as hot tears pricked her eyes like needles.

As Jace led his horse, Rascal, to the barn Wednesday evening, he spotted the red Maserati parked in Leah's drive. A frown furrowed his brow. He'd never seen that car there before. Wasting no time, he mounted Rascal and guided the stallion along the dusty trail beside the ranch house, across the highway, and on past the strange car. Hearing voices out back, he reined Rascal in to a walk, and as he came around the corner of Leah's house, he recognized the man with her. He was none too pleased by what he saw.

Leah and Johnny Enders were in the vegetable garden, talking and laughing across a row of black-eyed peas. Lifting his hat, Jace wiped his brow with the sleeve of his denim shirt before putting the Stetson back on. As Rascal strutted across the grassy back yard, Leah and Johnny noticed and turned to face them.

Feeling a mighty twinge in the area of her heart, Leah gathered in as deep a breath as possible and produced a smile. "Hi, Jace, what brings you here?"

"I didn't recognize the car. Thought it wouldn't hurt to check."

"How neighborly," she said, her expression innocent. She looked from Jace to Johnny and back again. "You two know each other, so I don't have to introduce you again."

"Right." Jace inclined his head at Enders. "Nice car you've got. Looks new."

"Bought her about a month ago," Johnny answered with great enthusiasm. "She's a dream to handle. And powerful—practically flies on a straightway."

Jace nodded politely and looked at Leah, his gaze capturing hers. For an uncomfortable time that seemed endless, they simply looked at each other as the tension grew. Johnny faked a cough, breaking the spell. He swept an arm out, smiling uneasily.

"Leah invited me to share in the bounty of her garden," he announced without being asked. "She's really got a green thumb, hasn't she? Look at all this."

"It's a great garden all right," Jace agreed evenly. "She's worked hard on it."

"Ah, but I can't take all the credit," she said, her expression composed and solemn. "You helped me plan it and plant it." She looked at Johnny. "Jace enjoys being neighborly."

The barely discernible sarcasm in her voice wasn't lost on Jace, although he doubted Enders noticed it. Shifting slightly in the saddle, Jace followed her with his eyes as she stepped carefully across the garden toward him, stopping to pull a carrot.

"Mind if I give it to Rascal?" she asked too politely, brushing the dirt from it. "I know he likes treats."

"And you know I don't mind if you give him one," Jace replied, his words clipped. "Carrots are good for him."

"Here boy," Leah murmured, rubbing the stallion's velvety nose, smiling as he nudged her hand. A large, powerful horse, he had fiery eyes and a spirit to match, but she had ridden him once and discovered he also knew how to be amazingly gentle. While he contentedly crunched the carrot between his teeth, she patted his neck, paying more attention to him than to his owner.

Jace dismounted and strode over to the edge of the garden, where Enders was bending over the rows of peas. "Need any help picking, Leah?"

"No thanks. We're nearly finished." Hooking her thumbs into the back pockets of her jeans she walked past Jace toward the tomato plants. "I'm giving him a little bit of everything. Decided I'd wait till next year to get into canning. By then the house should be all fixed up, and I'll have more time."

"Of course, I can't possibly eat all she's sending home with me. I'll share it with Marlene," Johnny said, adding for Jace's benefit, "Marlene's my sister."

"I know."

That short reply didn't exactly set the conversational ball rolling. No one said anything for several long minutes while Johnny picked peas and Leah yanked some weeds out of the ground.

"Well, if I can't be of help, I'll get going," Jace at last announced. "See you later, Leah. Enders."

"Wait," she called out as he turned back to Rascal. Picking up a large paper bag, she snapped it open with a flick of her wrist and started filling it with ripe tomatoes. When the sack was practically overflowing, she carried it over to Jace. "Take these home with you. Johnny doesn't want them all and I have plenty for myself. It would be a shame if they were wasted."

Nodding, he swung up into the saddle. When he reached down to take the bag she handed him, their fingers made brief contact. His gaze fixed on her upturned face and he saw her press her lips tightly together. For an instant, he considered sweeping her off her feet and riding away with her so they could be alone. But that wouldn't solve anything. He picked up the reins.

"Tell Cookie to come over anytime and pick what he wants from the garden," Leah added, trying to ignore the rapid beating of her heart. "He'll be doing me a favor."

"I'll tell him. Thanks." Jace tugged at the brim of his Stetson, issued a softly spoken command to Rascal, and rode away.

"Well, well, well," Johnny said as she turned to

face him. "For a man who says he doesn't want a commitment, he seemed to resent finding me here."

"What gave you that idea?"

"Bad vibes," Johnny joked. "Thought he was going to glare a hole right through me. If looks could kill . . ."

"I didn't notice anything like that."

"I'm sure he didn't intend you to. You know, you could use this to your advantage. If I start spending a lot of time with you, he might get jealous enough to—"

"No, Johnny, I'd never ask you to do that."

"You're not asking. I'm offering. Anything to serve the cause of true love."

Leah hesitated a second, truly tempted by the suggestion. At last she shook her head with firm resolution. "No. I'm not a game-player."

"It couldn't hurt to make him jealous."

"Maybe not. But I don't see how it would help, either." Pensively, she twirled a strand of hair in her fingers. "If he wants me back just because he thinks another man wants me, we wouldn't have the kind of relationship I need."

"Still, a good dose of jealousy might make him realize what he gave up."

"You're sweet, Johnny," she said, her smile wistful. "But surely it's occurred to you that maybe I just never meant all that much to him."

"I find that hard to believe."

"Flattery's precisely what I need. Keep it up," she teased, dusting off her hands. "Well, let's load this stuff into your car. Then we'll go in and have dinner."

"Sounds good to me. But I still have a feeling Jace

won't be very pleased if I stay much longer."

"That's his problem, then," Leah murmured, privately wondering if Jace cared enough to even notice when Johnny left her house.

CHAPTER EIGHT

Barefoot, clad in cutoffs and a T-shirt, Leah pulled herself off the sofa to answer the knock at her front door. Jace stood on the small porch, and his unexpected appearance did nothing to improve her already weak and weary condition. She simply couldn't face another confrontation with him at the moment. Transferring the damp folded cloth she held in one hand to the other, she sighed inwardly.

"Jace, I don't really feel—"

"I know. Buddy just told me that you weren't feeling well when he was over here early this afternoon," Jace said softly, examining her face closely. "Thought I'd better come see what's wrong."

"Oh, it's nothing much." She stepped aside automatically when he crossed the threshold decisively and entered the house. "It's just a granddaddy of a headache, that's all. I took a little nap. It's better now."

"Oh? You don't look so hot."

"It certainly isn't one of my finest hours. Thanks for reminding me."

"You know I wasn't insulting you," he admonished, touching the faint violet crescents under her eyes with feather-light fingertips. "I only meant you have dark circles here, and you look a little pale. Are you sure the headache's better? Got a fever?"

"No. Really, it doesn't hurt as much as it did."

"What brought it on?"

She shrugged. "Maybe it's all the dust in the air. I don't know. I'm just glad I didn't have any appointments this afternoon and was able to come home. Like I said, I slept a couple of hours and that helped a lot."

"But it didn't get rid of it completely. You look sort of shaky. Come on, sit down."

"No, I—Jace," she protested when he lightly took hold of her elbow. "I'm fine. You don't have to hold me up like I'm on my last legs or something."

He insisted, guiding her to the sofa and towering above her as she sank down at one end and tucked her bare legs up beside her. Compassion was easily readable in his eyes.

"A bad headache can really make you feel lousy. Anything I can get you?"

"I can't think of anything."

"Have you had dinner?"

"Not yet."

"Neither have I. I'll rustle up something for us."

"Jace, you don't have to." She touched his hand briefly as he started to walk away. 'I'm not very hungry. Don't go to the trouble."

"No trouble. I am hungry and you need to eat."

"But—"

"Hush," he murmured, tapping a silencing finger against her lips. "I'll go see what I can find in the kitchen. Don't expect an elaborate seven course meal on such short notice, though. It'll be something simple. Okay?"

She nodded, surrendering to his will. He intended to have his way and it wasn't worth her while to try to argue with him. Besides, she didn't want to argue about such an inconsequential matter. To do so would be a foolish waste of energy. Hearing him move around in the kitchen, she soaked the cloth she held in the steel basin of cold water she'd left on the coffee table, wrung it out, then applied it to her forehead. The pain had mercifully subsided to a dull ache. She didn't have headaches all that often, but when she did they were usually bad. It was so nice to feel this one slowly fading away. Closing her eyes, she leaned into the corner of the sofa and relaxed.

Jace returned to the parlor about fifteen minutes later and found Leah dozing. Stopping beside her, he looked down at her face. He hadn't seen her or talked to her for a week, since the evening Johnny Enders had visited. Enders. At the thought of the other man Jace's expression grew hard. Enders had stayed with her until after ten that night. Jace knew because he had watched and waited for him to leave.

Quietly, Jace placed the tray he was carrying on the table, straightening in time to see Leah's eyes flutter open and the sleepy smile that graced her lips. He bent down to stroke her hair back from her temples.

"You look better. Not so pale," he said. "Feeling any hungrier now?"

"Yes." She sat up. "That soup smells good. I love chicken noodle."

"Good." He settled down on the sofa beside her.

She ate all the soup in her bowl and half of the sandwich he'd made. Finished, she folded her napkin and replaced it on the tray.

"That was delicious, Jace, and you were right. I feel much better, now. Headache's nearly gone."

"See? I told you it would help," he taunted. "Maybe next time you won't try to argue with the advice I give. I know what makes people feel better."

"Oh?" Leah grinned. "And how did you get to be so wise?"

"My mother believed soup could cure just about anything that ailed you."

There was a sense of loss in his smile that tugged at Leah's heart. "You miss her very much, don't you?"

"Yes," he answered, his deep voice lowering. "I think everyone who knew her loved her. She was a special woman."

And she had raised a son who was special too. Jace was a fine man; he had a great capacity for caring that had made it easy for Leah to fall in love with him. Yet, knowing the kind of man he was just made it harder for her to handle the fact that he was unwilling to give her as much as she needed. She wished with all her heart it could be different for them. She wanted him so much that it hurt.

Slapping his thighs decisively, Jace stood. "Better wash the dishes."

"Just leave them. I'll do them in the morning."

"Nope. Can't let you wake up to dirty dishes."

She smiled up at him as he started past her. "You are the best neighbor I have, Jace."

"I'm the only one you have. Nobody else around for miles." He grinned. "But I'll accept that as a compliment anyway."

While he cleaned up the kitchen, Leah relaxed, relieved that her headache had faded. The effects of it still lingered, making her feel tired, but she knew a good night's sleep would remedy that. Hiding a yawn behind her hand, she looked up as Jace returned to the parlor.

"Maybe I should go," he suggested. "Let you get to bed."

"It's really too early for bed," she murmured, not wanting him to leave just yet, the need simply to be with him growing intense. "If I go to bed too early, I'll probably wake up in the middle of the night and not be able to go back to sleep."

"Even so, you'll be more relaxed if I'm not around."

She averted her eyes. "If you want to go . . ."

"Did I say I want to?" he muttered, his darkening gaze sweeping over her. In her shorts and clingy T-shirt she was casually alluring. Desire, never far from the surface where she was concerned, ran through his bloodstream, and he longed to hold her, make love with her for hours. "Did I?"

Tugging at a wayward wisp of her hair, she shook her head. "Does that mean you don't want to leave?"

"Hell, Leah," he growled, dropping down upon the sofa beside her and skimming one hand over her bare thigh. "I'm not sure I know what I want anymore."

She needed words of love, not uncertainty, and she moved his hand away as disappointment squeezed her heart. "Until you are sure, leave me alone, Jace."

"I don't seem to be able to do that," he whispered, gathering her into his arms, tilting up her chin, and lowering his mouth to cover hers.

Her lips parted. She was unable to stop herself from responding, until after a few dangerous moments logic managed to overcome emotion. She pulled away from him. "Jace, you can't have it both ways."

His face was hard as he asked, "You still don't understand why I have to be more careful this time, do you?"

"I . . . No, I guess I don't."

"Erica—"

"I told you I'm not Erica! I'm not at all like her. But maybe you're just using her as an excuse because you never really cared as much as I thought you did."

Getting up, Jace thrust his hands into his pockets and stared down at her. "You don't really believe that, do you?"

"How the devil should I know what to believe?" she retorted, waving him away from her. "It was nice of you to make dinner for me but I want you to leave now."

"All right. Fine."

"Fine."

" 'Night."

Leah didn't answer as he walked out the front door and closed it with a muted bang behind him. Crossing the road to his ranch, he glared up at the yellow full moon that should have been romantic but was instead merely taunting. He felt as ill-tempered as a hornet, disappointed in Leah's lack of understanding and aggravated by his own damnable, compulsive caution.

That weekend the hurricane lashing in the Gulf affected the weather throughout most of Texas. A seemingly never ending series of storms hit Dallas, Fort Worth, and the surrounding countryside. Torrents of rain beat at Leah's house Friday, Saturday, and Sunday, and by Sunday night she was wondering if she might be wise to start building an ark. At ten o'clock, while she was in the kitchen pouring a glass of iced tea, a bright flash of jagged lightning ripped through the sky, and she winced as a clap of thunder loud as a shotgun blast followed almost immediately. Then she heard the commotion in the henhouse, all the chickens clucking anxiously.

With a worried frown, she switched on the outside light and went to the window to peer through the darkness and rain at the coop, a barely visible shadowy shape. Lightning flashed again and she gasped as she saw it reflected in the water that completely surrounded it. The creek had been close to overflowing its banks all day but she hadn't expected it to rise this fast. If only she had moved the coop farther up the small hill when she'd repaired it... But she hadn't.

"A veritable flood," she mumbled, knowing she had to go to the chickens' rescue. From the hall closet she got out her raincoat and put it on over the shorts and top she wore. Piling her hair on top of her head, she pulled her rain hat down to her ears and looked down at her tennis shoes, shrugging. "One of these days, you have to buy some rain boots," she told herself.

She got a flashlight from the kitchen and she went out into the night, pushing against the roaring wind and the rain driving down in sheets. Her serviceable raincoat was not really adequate protection against the wild weather, and before she got far from the house, dampness was already seeping through the lining. Suddenly, a powerful gust of wind snatched her hat off her head She tried to chase it down but it kept spinning out of reach, so she soon gave up. Her hair was soaked by now anyway.

Three-quarters of the way down the incline, she waded gingerly into the floodwater, grimacing as it swirled turgidly around her ankles. By the time she opened the gate in the wire fence, it was lapping against her calves and she was happy to climb the three wooden steps to the entrance of the coop. She shone the flashlight inside and saw the chickens flapping their wings and nervously fluttering around. The sound of the storm drowned out everything but their wild clucking, and she wasn't prepared for the hand that suddenly clamped her shoulder.

"You and your damn chickens," Jace swore, his face stony, as he spun her around to face him. "What do you think you're doing out here?"

"Having a picnic. What does it look like?" she snapped, angry at him for sneaking up on her and for his tone of voice. "What are you doing here?"

"I saw your outside lights go on and then the flashlight beam, so I knew you were up to something. But you didn't answer my question. What are you doing?"

"I saw the creek was up. I had to check the chickens, didn't I?"

"Why?" he asked, gesturing with his free hand. "They're all right, just a little jumpy because of the storm. And the coop's two feet off the ground. The water's not going to get that high. Even if it did, they could roost in the rafters."

"Well, I didn't think of that. I thought maybe I should move them up to the shed."

"Do you know how many trips that would take you? For God's sake, Leah, would you really risk getting struck by lightning for these chickens?"

"I don't have to listen to you preach me a sermon," she said coldly, moving past him down the steps and sloshing through the water. He caught up with her and roughly picked her up in his arms. She squirmed. "What—"

Tennis shoes," he grumbled when he saw her feet. "You came out here in tennis shoes? I can't believe it. Why didn't you put on boots?"

"I don't have any. Now put me down, I can walk."

"All right," he said, and started to lower her to the ground, "but you never know what the creek has washed up. If you aren't worried about a water moccasin wrapping around your leg..."

She wound her arms tightly around his neck, shuddering with revulsion at the thought. "Okay, okay, I'll let you carry me."

"Thanks a lot," he drawled sardonically.

Lightning lit up the sky as they reached higher ground. He put her down, grabbed her hand, and made a mad dash for the house. Booming thunder rattled the windows as they ran around the house to the porch, where he pulled off his waterproof poncho and dropped it to the floor. Except for the bottoms of his pants legs he was dry, but Leah was drenched. She wiped the rain from her face, touched her dripping hair, and struggled to untie the wet belt of her raincoat.

"You're soaked clear through," Jace murmured, helping her peel that garment off. "All for a few chickens. Little idiot."

"I am not an idiot."

"Loco then."

"I'm not crazy either," she said through clenched teeth, color rising in her cheeks. "But if you want to start a namecalling contest, I certainly have a few I could call you."

"Be very careful," Jace warned, his voice and the touch of his hand on her arm deceptively soft, at variance with the steely glint in his eyes. "I'm running out of patience."

"You are?" She tossed up her head. "Well, let me tell you something, cowboy, my patience with you ended a long time ago. Besides, I didn't ask you to come over here tonight."

"What choice did I have once I knew you were outside?" he countered, towering above her. "I didn't know what you were up to. If you'd waded much deeper you might have been caught in an undertow and pulled out into the creek."

"Surely you don't think I'd be stupid enough to let the current get me."

"Frankly, I'm not always sure what you might do, a city girl trying to live the country life."

"What a rotten thing to say!" she heatedly exclaimed, her hands closing in tight fists. "I'm not *trying* to live this life. I do live it and I've learned how to take care of—"

"Oh, go get out of those clothes," Jace commanded, taking her arm and bringing her through the door. "Go dry off."

"Why don't you dry up?" she responded under her breath, heading for the stairs.

Up in the bathroom, she pulled off her soggy tennis shoes and shed her shirt and shorts. Jace was right. She was soaked clear through. Even her bra and panties clung clammily to her skin, and it felt good to be rid of them and to rub her body down with a thick towel. After squeezing the water out of her hair and rubbing it partially dry, she slipped into her short white robe. Just as she started down the hall to her room for fresh clothes, lightning flashed, thunder crashed, and the entire house was plunged into darkness.

"Terrific, no electricity." Sliding her hand over the wall, she guided herself along.

"Got any lanterns? Candles?" Jace shouted up the stairwell.

"In the pantry on the right-hand side," she called back. "If you can't find them I'll be down in a minute."

She found her door and felt her way across the room, helped once by an opportune streak of lightning, which illuminated everything for a second. She opened the drawer of her bedside table, took out the flashlight she kept there, and flicked it on. Nothing happened. She rapped it lightly with her palm. Still nothing. Obviously it needed new batteries. She sighed and started to leave the room, stubbing her toe on the foot of the antique dresser.

"Hellfire," she softly swore, bent over, balancing on one leg as she rubbed the injured foot.

"What have you done now?" Jace asked from the top of the stairs, and came into the room carrying a kerosene lantern. He put it down on top of the dresser and took hold of her right elbow. "What's the matter?"

"Oh, I just jammed my toe."

"Think it's broken?"

"No. It's already feeling better. You know how painful it is when you first stub your toe," she said, extracting her arm from his grip and lowering her foot to the floor again. "It's fine."

When she looked up at him, his gaze imprisoned hers. In the wavering lantern light, their shadows danced on the walls. Outside the storm raged, the rain peppered down, and the wind shrieked through the trees. But the room was cool and cozy and bathed in a golden glow. Wisps of Leah's drying flaxen hair framed her face and the lantern's glow was reflected in her jade green eyes. She was so fresh, so lovely to look at. The light robe she wore was practically translucent; the shape of her body a silhouette of rounded curves, insweeping waist, and shapely thighs. Jace's mouth went dry. His pulse rate accelerated, and he couldn't help looking at her. Or touching her. Reaching out, he brushed her hair back from her temples.

Danger signals clamored in her head as her heart seemed to do a crazy little somersault. She took a small backward step. "Let's go downstairs," she suggested, managing not to sound as breathless as she suddenly felt. "Without electricity we can't have coffee, but I have some brandy."

As she moistened her lips with the tip of her tongue, Jace moved closer to her. "Leah."

"No. Jace, don't." Unable to disguise the unsteadiness in her voice this time, she pushed at his chest as he relentlessly pulled her toward him. "Stop."

"I can't," he whispered, his lips gliding across her smooth cheek toward her mouth. "I want you, honey."

"*No.*"

"Yes, Leah."

"But, Jace, you said—"

"Hush now." Pressing her hands hard against his chest, he eased the edge of his own hand between her round breasts. "Feel how fast my heart's beating? Yours is beating like crazy too."

It was, but she forced herself to put up a struggle. "Jace, let me go."

"No. I can't now."

"You *have* to. I know you. You wouldn't force me to . . ."

"I won't have to force you," he murmured, his breath hot and enticing upon her skin. "You've missed what we had together as much as I have."

A low moan escaped her throat. Her brain screamed at her to deny him, but that would have meant also denying herself. Her body turned traitor as his long fingers coursed over her, fiery and firm, igniting her nerve endings, drawing outward all the love she had tried to bury deep in her heart. Now it burst forth again in blooming passion and the natural need to give, weakening the remains of her inner resistance and dissolving them utterly.

She loved him too much; touching and being touched by him was such a delight. The feel of his lithe, virile body inflamed her senses, made her dizzy. His sculpted lips grazed over hers, seeking, arousing. Raw aching need exploded volcanically in the very center of her being and flowed through her veins. She guided her hands up under the tail of his shirt, over the broad expanse of his chest.

"Leah," he said huskily, encouraging her. "You do want me as much as I want you, don't you?"

"Yes," she breathlessly confessed, quickly clasping her arms together around his neck. Sweet anticipation rushed through her as he started to undo the belt of her robe. She knew the ecstasy had only begun.

CHAPTER NINE

Aching for the delight they always shared in intimacy, aroused by the power of her love, she unbuttoned his shirt, slowly stepping her fingertips over his chest as she did so, skimming her nails through the fine dark hair there. The rain beat against the windowpanes, the storm enclosing them in a world of their own. She pushed his shirt off his broad shoulders and he shrugged out of it, his eyes never leaving hers as he removed her robe and gave it a careless toss. Then his caressing gaze lowered.

"I love to look at you."

"I love it when you do."

"Exhibitionist."

"Only for you."

"Damn right," he growled, his smile provocative. "You're mine, honey."

She knew she was. He was the man she wanted and loved and it was good to give herself to him. The look in his eyes as they wandered over her was so passionately intent that she felt as aroused as if she had actually been touched. "You make me feel so . . . desirable."

"Because you are," said Jace softly. "Come here, woman."

She stepped closer, the catch in her breath audible when he slipped his hands beneath her hair and took hold of her shoulders. His thumbs feathered up her neck to lift her chin. Her lips parted, but his only played over the corners of her mouth again and again, teasing and enticing. She rested her arms on his shoulders, caressed the rims of his ears, then stretched up to nibble at one lobe.

His own breathing quickened. "That drives me crazy."

"Mmm, I know."

"Be careful," he cautioned wickedly. "Two can play this game."

"You started it, with those tiny little kisses."

"You mean like these?" His hard mouth began toying with hers once more. "Hmm?"

"Yeah . . . like . . . those," she managed to murmur between kisses. Wrapping her arms around his waist, she leaned back against his supporting arm as he explored her face by touch, his fingers tenderly following the arch of her eyebrows, the delicate curve of her jaw, the slight hollows beneath her cheekbones. A very real gentleness tempered the glint of desire in his magnificent blue eyes, and her love for him knew no limits. Thunder rumbled outside, but in the room hushed silence enveloped them as they stood in the golden circle of the lantern's glow.

"Smile," Leah whispered, dancing her fingertips over the tiny dimples that etched his cheeks when he did. His skin was smooth, deeply bronzed, and she explored the planes of his face as if committing his carved features to memory.

Her soft caresses drew a tortured moan from him. Capturing her hand, he flicked the tip of his tongue over her palm and nibbled on the tender mound of flesh at the base of her thumb.

She trembled. "That drives me crazy."

"Mmm, I know," he answered, giving her own words back to her. "That's why I'm doing it." He pressed her fingers against his chest, lowering his head to brush his lips over the faint shadows beneath her eyes. "You still have light circles there. Haven't you been sleeping well?"

"Not every night."

"Me either."

Had he lain awake, thinking about her? She had, thinking about him. Missing him. Wishing... But she didn't want to remember those restless, lonely hours right now. Tonight he was with her, and she wanted to lose herself in what they would share together. Only the present mattered. Stroking his hair, she pressed closer, her scalp tingling when he ran his strong fingers through the still damp thickness of her own hair. Then his hands prowled hotly over her, floating down her back to the base of her spine, to cup her firm bottom and arch her against him.

He let her go only to take hold of her hand and lead her to the bed, where he wasted no time throwing back the covers. He sat down on the edge, his dark eyebrows rising quizzically when she held back as he tried to pull her to him.

"I'll help you with your boots," she explained, sinking to her knees on the oval hooked rug. Looking up at him, she made a great show of batting her lashes, playing the coquette. "Mother told me men like to be pampered sometimes."

"Lucky man, your father." Grinning, Jace pulled his feet out as she tugged.

After removing his socks, she extended her hands high above her head and bowed from the waist, practically touching her nose to the floor. "Master," she intoned, fighting a giggle before succumbing to temptation and tickling his toes.

Yanking his feet back out of her reach, he grasped her shoulders. "Come here, slave girl," he commanded, lifting her up between his legs to stand before him. His gaze devoured her. Her skin glowed, her limbs lightly tanned, the rest of her ivory, untouched by the rays of the sun. She was lovely.

"Thank goodness, you're not all skin and bones," he murmured unevenly, his deep-timbered voice lowering. "Too many women these days look like they're half starved."

"I doubt I'll ever look like that. Plumpness runs in my family."

"You're not plump."

"When I get older I probably will be."

"So?"

"So what's the use fighting heredity?" she retorted, cradling his beloved face in her hands. "When I gain a little weight, I'll have an excuse to buy a whole new wardrobe. Now I've told you my family secret. Don't you have one to tell me to make us even?"

His eyes narrowed, surveying her suspiciously. "Sue told you, didn't she? That's why you're asking. She told you about Dad?"

Thoroughly confused, Leah shook her head.

"What about him?"

"Baldness. His hair started getting thin when he hit forty. Mine will too, I suppose."

"Aw, that is a tragedy," she said, trying not to laugh at his comical expression. She shrugged. "Well, you should have told me sooner. I would have known better than to get involved with—"

"Too late," he whispered, lowering her hands to his belt. "What we've started, we have to finish."

Heart racing with excitement, she undid the belt buckle and waited breathlessly as he stripped. Curving her fingers over his powerful shoulders, she urged him down upon the bed, moving above him, reveling in the taut strength of his thighs between hers.

Raw need erupted in him, blazing hot and clamoring for release. Too soon. He wanted, needed to prolong the ecstasy, knowing that building the anticipation would make completion all the better for both of them. Clasping her waist, he lifted her higher above him, raining kisses over her free, full breasts.

She wriggled closer, moving sinuously, every nerve coming gloriously alive as iron hard masculinity surged against her, stirring over the sensitive skin of her abdomen. Enthralled by the fresh male scent of him, transported by his touch, she felt as if she were literally melting into him, her flesh becoming his while his became hers.

"Jace," she breathed, her parted lips finding his as she dropped kiss after kiss upon them, her tongue daring to seek the warm rough surface of his.

"I'm your slave too, honey. Leah, my sweet Leah," he crooned softly, coaxingly pushing his tongue into her mouth, rubbing the tip over the inner flesh of her cheek and feeling the shiver that rushed over her as he did.

Her senses swirled as his kisses deepened to become erotic preludes of ultimate intimacy, his tongue, his teeth, and his masterful lips creating an endless series of undulating thrills that coursed through her. Rippling sensations far beyond her control set her on fire, and the heat leapt outward from the very center of her being. Turning her head from side to side, she ardently encouraged the fine chain of golden kisses he laced around her neck. His warm lips lingered on the skittering pulse in her throat, his even teeth nipped her skin. She rested her entire weight upon him, luxuriating in his physical strength as his muscular arms tightened around her. He turned, pressed her down into the soft mattress, the compelling weight of his torso heavy on her yielding breasts.

He felt her nipples surge warmly against him and the longing to touch, to taste, overwhelmed him. He reverently cupped the enticing weight of her breasts in his hands, his palms slowly rotating, his fingers squeezing and caressing her satinesque skin. Her velvet green eyes met his; her lush moist lips were parted. He bent his head. Her slender fingers tangled in his hair as he kissed the rosy peaks of her womanly flesh, one after the other, repeatedly, then sampled their honeyed sweetness with his tongue and closing his mouth possessively around one and then the other.

Leah gasped, drowning in delight as his mouth sketched tantalizing patterns on her. She cried out softly as he hungrily drew deeper on her nipples, plundering their aroused erectness. Tightly, she clasped her arms together over the small of his back, beseeching him, "Take me. Oh Jace, take me now. Love me."

"Soon. I'll have to soon," he uttered hoarsely, scarcely able to hold his own desire in check as she languidly moved one thigh between his legs. "But I don't want it to end too soon. I need hours with you, Leah. All night. With you in this bed. My darlin' Leah."

"Oh Jace, I—"

He kissed her, catching her words with his mouth. She arched toward him, responsive and eager. He had to have all of her: body, soul, and mind, freely given. Never before in his life had he felt this way about any woman. Leah gave much more than mere physical pleasure, she gave him joy too. She was irresistible. Easing between her shapely legs, he parted her thighs with the outward pressure of his.

When he touched her there, a soft moan of delight swept out between her parted lips, and she touched him. Turning over, her nearly dry hair cascaded forward, framing her face and tickling him as she scattered kisses over his shoulders and chest, his abdomen and thighs while her hands stroked and caressed.

Breathing faster, he cupped her breasts, squeezing gently. Her answering sigh fluttered over his skin, fueling the fire of his passion.

"I need you so much," he groaned, pulling her beneath him once again. "I have to have you now. I can't wait."

"Love me," she repeated, parting her legs wider, linking her fingers with his as he held her hands down upon the pillow. Her dreamy eyes searched the depths of his. He was poised above her, muscular arms fully extended, and she felt the hard pressure of him throb against her.

As she lifted her hips, he thrust gently inside, claiming her warmth, immersing himself in her, hearing their soft sounds of mutual satisfaction mingle. He saw bliss in her face and smiled tenderly. She smiled back, her lips curving sensuously.

Never had she felt so close to him in spirit. Lovingly, she began to move, and as he moved with her, his slow rousing strokes enhanced the pleasure. One moment flowed into another, and another, becoming a timeless stream of exquisite sensation and emotion. United as one, they touched and kissed and created a storm of feelings that rivaled the one raging outside. Jace worshipped her with his hands, his lips, his whole body, and she clung to him, holding him deep inside her. He felt her quiver as passion mounted in both of them, rushing toward the pinnacle. Suddenly he was still, then withdrew, despite her soft protest. He feathered his fingers between her thighs, exploring the warmth his body had just left, fondling the contours of womanly flesh with artful caresses. Her softly glowing eyes met the penetrative glint in his as she guided him back to her and he entered once again. Possessing each other their heated bodies, perfectly attuned, moved in wondrous synchronization, carrying them higher and higher, close to the ultimate peak until he was still within her once more.

"*Jace*," she whispered, holding him tighter, kissing his neck and the pulse pounding in his throat. Her hands swept feverishly over his buttocks.

Unable to prolong the lovemaking any longer, he

took her, thrusting harder and faster, feeling her flutter and strain against him as completion came and he joined her in it.

Waves of piercing release crested, subsided, then crested again, suspending them both for several dazzling moments on the finely honed edge of fulfillment. Then they tumbled down together and lay, limbs entwined, in the tangle of sheets.

Outside the flashes of lightning were no longer so bright; thunder still rumbled, but from a distance. Sighing contentedly, Leah snuggled closer to Jace, closing her eyes, resting her hand on his chest. After their heart rates returned to normal, she stirred only once.

"I love you," she murmured as she fell asleep.

Silently, Jace brushed her tousled hair back from her temples and placed a lingering kiss on her brow.

Leah woke up early and rose to put on her robe. Then she sat down on the edge of the bed beside Jace. Still asleep, he had flung one arm across her pillow and was sprawled out on his back. She smiled to herself. She could see more of the boy he'd once been in his relaxed features, and lightly touched the shock of dark brown hair tumbling across his forehead. A day's growth of beard shadowed his jaw, and she rubbed the faint stubble with one fingertip before bending down to whisper into his ear, "You're snoring."

"Wh—what?" Forcing his eyes open he looked blearily at her. "Did you say I was snoring?"

"Just kidding."

"Oh." He rubbed his hand over his face. "Good."

"Mornin'," she murmured, brushing her mouth against his. Sleepy as he was, he responded instantly, his lips demanding, his arms starting to go around her. Laughing, she pulled away and ran from the bed, tossing back the challenge, "Catch me if you can."

"Oh, I will," he retorted, smiling. He flung off the covers, lowered his feet to the floor, and she took off like a shot, her robe billowing out behind her as she ran down the hall. Laughing too, Jace gave chase. He almost caught her in the kitchen, but she managed to get away by faking to the right and cutting left, thus getting by him and out the door to the foyer. At last he cornered her in the parlor. With lissome grace, she tried to slip between the sofa and the wall, but he was too fast for her. His hands shot out, securing hers, and he drew her around the end of the couch to face him.

"And now that I've captured you, what's my prize?"

She turned her eyes up at him. "Your wish is my command."

"Dangerous promise," he told her as he picked her up. He threw her over one shoulder and headed back upstairs.

Considerably later, Jace watched her stretch like a lazy kitten and sit up in bed, the sheet draping her breasts. She yawned. "Much as I hate to say this, we have to get up," she declared, biting back another yawn that tried to follow the first. "We both have to work today."

"Yes," he drawled, fighting a grin and losing. "You've already kept me away from my cattle for over an hour, woman."

She laughed merrily. "I do hope you'll forgive me."

"I guess it was worth it."

She poked him in the ribs. Holding the sheet around her, she leaned sideways to lift the corner of the curtain and peek out the window. "Drizzling. And the sky still looks mean, with swirling clouds. I hope my chickens are okay."

"They're fine." He laid his hands on her bare back. "It rained hard after I found you out there, but not enough to flood the henhouse."

"I wonder if the storm blew down my corn?"

"Wouldn't doubt it. But I'm sure most of the roots are still in the ground. If it's down, I'll help you stake it back—"

The phone on the bedside table rang. Leah answered it and then handed the receiver to him. "It's Buddy."

Jace greeted him and began to listen, and she saw him tense, the muscles in his face tight and his narrowing eyes turning steely gray. She gazed worriedly at him. The moment he hung up, she blurted out, "What's the matter? Bad news?"

"Yes," he answered, his deep melodious voice acquiring a grating edge. "Erica just called from the airport. She's on her way out here."

Moaning inwardly, Leah began twisting a strand of her hair. "She's coming home? Why?"

"She's coming, but not home. It isn't her home anymore," Jace said flatly. "And I have no idea why she decided to return. But it won't take me long to head her right back to the airport. Hell, I better get over there before she arrives."

"How is she going to get here?"

"She rented a car. That's all she told Buddy."

"Jace," Leah murmured as he started to move off the bed, the question tumbling out before she could prevent it, "will I see you tonight?"

A muscle worked in his jaw. "I don't know."

Her heart sank. "Last night and this morning didn't change your mind, did it? You didn't intend—"

"I'm not sorry it happened."

"But you still don't want to be seriously involved with anybody, even me. Right?"

"Leah . . ."

"Oh damn," she muttered, turning away from him.

"Honey, it's just bad timing for that particular question," he tried to explain, feeling terrible when he touched her shoulder and she flinched. "With Erica on the way, I—"

"To hell with Erica. And to hell with you too. I'm tired of this roller coaster, Jace. Go away."

"If that's what you want."

"It is," she lied, struggling to steady her voice and miraculously succeeding. "You'd better hurry before she arrives. God knows, I don't want her barging in here."

Jace sighed. "We can talk about this later."

Doubting he'd want to, she didn't bother to answer. He got dressed and kissed her. She didn't respond.

"Leah, what else can I say right now?"

"How about good-bye?" she replied stiffly, and meant it. Yet when he left, banging the door shut on his way out, she sobbed. Tears freely fell as she scrambled out of bed, showered quickly, and dressed. She practically ran out of the house, eager to start for the studio before Erica could have a chance to drop by for a visit. Having to see that woman would have been the last straw.

CHAPTER TEN

"I told you I'd help you do that." Jace walked into Leah's garden where she was working with the corn stalks and long wooden stakes. She continued what she was doing without looking up, but that didn't stop him from taking the hammer out of her hand. "Here, I'll put the stakes in the ground and you can tie up the stalks. We can leave the ones that aren't too low; they'll straighten up on their own."

She gnawed her bottom lip in silence as they worked together. The storm had beaten down the cornstalks, but they were still firmly rooted, and it was fairly easy to tie up the plants so that they reached for the sun again. With Jace's help, whether or not she wanted it, progress was swiftly made. Finally, she had to ask, "What did Erica want?"

"Money."

"Oh."

"I gave her some and sent her on her way."

"Think she'll be back?"

"I told her not to waste my time or hers by trying. The divorce settlement was generous. Unfortunately, she's spent all of it."

Leah absorbed that information in silence. When he pounded in the last stake and she carefully tied the stalk to it with a strip of an old bed sheet, she searched her brain for something to say to him, coming up empty. He had hurt her, was hurting her right now, and he knew it, which made her uncomfortable with him. Sometimes she wished they had remained simply neighbors. But fate had taken a hand and now... She swallowed with difficulty.

"There," she murmured, tightening the last knot a bit. "Thanks for helping."

"You're welcome."

"I think maybe the whole crop can be saved."

"Looks like it. Chickens okay?"

"Fine, like you said. But it's still so cloudy. Looks like we might have another storm tonight. I'm beginning to wonder if it'll ever stop raining."

"It will when the hurricane dies down."

They were reduced to talking about the weather! Feeling a great sense of loss she headed for the house, never once glancing at him. At the back door, she tried valiantly to still the hope rising in her heart as she politely asked, "Want a beer?"

"No thanks, Leah. Better go on home now."

She looked down at the ground. All his doubts about them were still there, and despite what he had said he wasn't willing to discuss their relationship. Maybe he never would be. He didn't love and want her as much as she loved and wanted him. That was a fact, pure and simple—one she would have to learn to accept. With a painful knot lodged solidly in her chest, she opened the door and went in.

"See you later, Leah," he said quietly.

"Jace," she was compelled to call after him as he started to walk away. He turned back and her own self-respect spurred her on. "If you don't want a serious involvement, if you're afraid of commitment, that's your problem. But don't expect me to be a convenient bed partner whenever you're in the mood, just because I live right across the road. I won't be used that way."

He shook his head. "Leah, you know you mean more to me than that."

"I don't know what I mean to you. I'm not sure I know you at all," she said, and went into the house.

During the rest of the week, Leah avoided Jace. He knew she did so deliberately, and couldn't really blame her, but he missed her like crazy; her warmth, her laughter, her giving nature. Days, he could keep busy, but nights were spent restlessly roaming his house and looking out frequently at her lighted windows. He debated endlessly with himself: was he wise to remain cautious, or was he taking a chance of letting someone very precious slip through his fingers? Erica was Erica. Leah was a completely different woman. He didn't want to risk losing her, yet his marriage to Erica had been such a bitter disappointment. He didn't want to risk that happening again, especially so soon after the first experience. But he truly missed being with Leah.

She didn't come home Friday night. He listened for her car, but never heard it. He watched for her lights to go on but they never did. Was she spending another weekend in town? Probably, but he couldn't be sure and couldn't even ask Buddy if he knew where she was—the foreman had gone into Irving to celebrate his sister's birthday, and wouldn't be back until the next day. Raking his fingers through his hair, Jace went to pour himself a drink, hoping the night wouldn't drag by too slowly and that he'd be able to get some sleep.

When Buddy drove his old truck in just after eleven Saturday morning, Jace met him in the barnyard.

"Do you know where Leah is?" he asked as the ranch foreman climbed out of the cab. "She did ask you to take care of her chickens, didn't she?"

"Yep. Said I'd be glad to."

"Well, did she tell you where she was going to spend the weekend?"

"Nope, didn't say nothing about where. Just that she'd be gone all week."

"All week?" Jace repeated, his frown deepening. "If she knew she was going to be gone that long, she could have at least told one of us where she'd be."

Tipping his hat far back on his head, Buddy regarded him solemnly. "Reckon she might've just forgot to mention it," he finally suggested, but he wasn't too surprised when Jace shook his head. "Maybe she thought it wouldn't matter to us where she went."

"It matters to me."

"Yep, I can see that," Buddy replied, reaching for a cigarette. He offered one to Jace, and lit them both with one match. He looked down at the ground. "You can tell me to mind my own business if you want to. I ain't much of one for giving advice, but I have a little for you if you want it."

"Why not? I think I could use some."

"Well, it's like this. I had a good woman once, couple of years before I came to work here. But I didn't think I'd ever want to settle down in one place back then, so I let her get away from me. Worst mistake I ever made. Hate to see you make the same one with Leah."

"I'd hate that, too, but it's not as simple as you think."

"Shoot, Jace, nothing worthwhile's apt to be simple. Leah's a good woman. That Erica was all wrong for you," Buddy said. "Leah ain't one bit like her."

"I know she isn't."

"Well then, that's all I wanted to say."

Nodding thoughtfully, Jace muttered, "I just wish I knew where she is right now."

"Reckon you'll just have to wait and ask her where she's been when she gets back."

"I'm not willing to wait that long."

"Thought not," was Buddy's brief answer. He blew a perfect smoke ring and ambled away.

Jace went into the house and called the Carousel Boutique in Fort Worth, but Marlene was out of town for the day and the clerk left in charge had no idea where Leah had gone. Undaunted, he dialed Johnny Enders's number but no one answered, and he hung up the receiver with more force than was necessary. Then he remembered Leah's parents. Maybe she had gone to visit them, and even if she hadn't they almost certainly knew where she was. There was only one problem; their phone number in Austin was unlisted. But he wasn't going to let a little detail like that stop him. He knew where Leah hid a spare house key. Maybe she had the number written down.

Five minutes later, he let himself into the quiet house and immediately found her address book in her desk.

"Damn," he muttered when he discovered the number he sought wasn't there. But his eye was caught by the letter next to the lamp. It was from Leah's mother and the return address said Lone Pond, Texas. Not Austin, which was where he had called last time for directory assistance. Maybe if he asked for a listing for Zeb Bancroft in Lone Pond he'd get lucky. It certainly was worth a chance.

Jace went home to place the call and the operator promptly gave him the number. After thanking her, he broke the connection and dialed Lone Pond, drumming his fingers impatiently as the phone rang ten or eleven times. He was about to give up and try again later when a man finally answered.

He plunged right in. "Mr. Bancroft, this is Jace Austin. Leah's neighbor across the road."

"Oh yes, Jace, we met you when we visited Leah last fall. How're you doing?"

"Fine. I—"

"Of course we were there when the house was still a mess. She tells us the old place is really shaping up. Sent us a few pictures of the rooms she's redecorated. They looked good."

"Yes, she's done a magnificent job fixing the house up," Jace hastily assured him, in no mood for small talk. "The reason I called is that I'm trying to locate Leah. I figured you'd know where she is."

"She's here. Flew in last night. She's going to spend the week with us."

Heaving a silent sigh of relief, Jace rubbed his

forehead. "I thought she might be there."

"I'm surprised you didn't know. Seems to me she said she asked you to feed her chickens while she's gone."

"No. She asked my ranch foreman, but she didn't tell him where she planned to go."

"Uh-huh. Well, is something wrong at her place? Is that why you're calling?"

"No, nothing's wrong. I ... Could I speak to her for a moment?"

Zeb Bancroft chuckled. "When I said she was here, I meant she's here with us, but she's not actually in the house at the moment. She's with her mother over at an aunt's house. They should be back in an hour or so. Can I give her a message?"

"No. No message." Jace spoke quietly. "I really only wanted to know where she was."

"I'll tell her you called."

"Thank you."

"Would you like her to call you when she gets in, Jace?"

There was dead silence on the line for a moment before the answer came back. "I'll leave that up to her."

"I see," Leah's father muttered, though he sounded as if he didn't understand at all.

After thanking him once more, Jace said good-bye, hung up, and walked out onto his front porch. Now at least he knew exactly where she was and that she was safe. That made him feel better. Yet ... His troubled gaze drifted across the road. Her house was going to look very lonely without her in it for the next week.

"Dang!" Zeb Lancroft exclaimed, hitting his forehead with the heel of his hand as they finished dinner Saturday night. "I was mowing the grass when you two got back from Sally's and I plain forgot to tell you Jace Austin called, Leah."

Her heart flip-flopped. Twisting her napkin in her lap, she stared at her father with disbelieving eyes. "Jace called here?"

"Far as I could tell, he just wanted to know if you were here. Why didn't you tell him you were spending your vacation with us?"

"I . . . didn't get a chance to."

"You had a chance to tell his foreman when you asked him to feed the chickens."

She made a small gesture and uttered a little white lie. "I forgot to mention it. Did Jace say anything else?"

"Just that you'd really done a lot fixing up that old house of yours. Of course, I brought that subject up."

"And that's all he said?" Leah persisted, feeling the warmth in her cheeks and knowing color was rising in them. Why did even the mention of Jace's name have to affect her? She wasn't an infatuated teenager, although lately she sometimes felt as confused as one. Struggling to pull herself together, she mustered a weak smile for her parents. "He didn't say anything else at all?"

"Well, I asked him if there was some problem at your place and he said there wasn't. But if you're worried maybe you should give him a call."

"Did he ask you to have me call him back?"

"Not exactly," Zeb replied, exchanging a puzzled glance with his wife Emily. "He said it was up to you whether or not you called him."

The tiny bubble of hope that had been expanding slowly in her popped and collapsed. She nodded. "I see."

"Are you? Going to call him back, I mean?"

"No."

"Maybe you should. He—"

"I don't want to," she said much more sharply than she meant to, then shrugged apologetically. "Sorry. I didn't mean to snap."

"Sweetheart, what's bothering you?" her mother asked with rare bluntness. "You haven't really been yourself since you got here last night. I told Zeb something was wrong when we went to bed, didn't I, Zeb? You're too quiet, Leah. And now I have a feeling the reason you are has something to do with Jace Austin."

"So do I," Zeb concurred, a worried frown darkening his brow. "What's going on, Leah?"

She shrugged again, this time rather wearily. "I don't really want to talk about it right now. Maybe later."

"Now," her father gently insisted. "Come on, kiddo, spill the beans."

She smiled tremulously at his old nickname for her. "You two certainly can see right through me, can't you?"

"Of course we can," Emily Bancroft said, patting her daughter's shoulder. "Tell us what's wrong. Maybe we can help."

"I don't think so, not this time," she murmured, but she knew she owed them the truth. "I'm in love with Jace, but he doesn't want to be seriously involved with anybody right now."

A thunderous expression crossed Zeb's face. "Are

you saying he's been dallying with your affections?"

Unhappy as she felt, she had to laugh a little. "Oh Dad, what an old-fashioned way to put it."

"I don't care how old-fashioned I sound. Has he?"

"Yes, I guess he has in a way. But I'm not sure he meant to."

"I'm tempted to take the next plane to Fort Worth and drive out to his ranch," said Zeb, exhibiting a father's protective instincts. "I'd like to have a nice long chat with that young man. Nobody hurts one of my daughters and gets away with—"

"Shh, dear, calm down," Emily interceded, patting his arm. "We don't even know all the facts yet. Leah, what about Erica, Jace's wife?"

"Ex-wife."

"Yes, I know. You told me they were divorced. Does she have anything to do with this?"

Mothers are often amazingly wise and incredibly perceptive. "I guess Erica has everything to do with it," Leah admitted, releasing her breath in a rush. "Jace says marrying her was the biggest mistake he ever made and now he wants to be very careful about making another commitment."

"Leah, for goodness' sake, how many times did I tell you and Lynn to steer clear of married and divorced men?" Emily brusquely inquired, proving also that mothers can occasionally speak words that wound without intending to. "Why didn't you listen to me?"

Catching her lower lip between her teeth, Leah stood. "Saying 'I told you so' isn't very helpful, Mother," she muttered, turning on her heel. She maintained her dignified posture as she went down the hall toward her old room. Once she closed the door behind her, however, her shoulders sagged and she flung herself across the bed, tears stinging her eyes. She blinked them back as Zeb followed, knocked once, and came in to sit down beside her.

He stroked her back. "Your mother didn't mean that, kiddo. She's just hurt because you are and she didn't know what else to say."

"I—I know," Leah murmured haltingly. "It's okay."

"Is it, Leah? You aren't in trouble, are you?"

Turning over she smiled lovingly at him and shook her head. "You're sounding old-fashioned again but no, I'm not pregnant, Dad."

"Good. I wouldn't want to have to get my shotgun out and go after Jace Austin," he said, attempting a joke. But his somber face betrayed him as he patted her shoulder. "I'm sorry you're not happy, baby."

"Me too, but I'll live through it."

"Sure you will. Bancrofts are tough."

"Survivors," she agreed, sitting up to kiss his cheek, smelling the familiar comforting scent of his aftershave. "I'll be fine."

"I know you will. And maybe it will all work out. After all, Jace did call to make sure you were here."

"I don't want to raise false hopes just because he did that, Dad. He knows how to be a good neighbor. That might be all his call meant. I guess I should have told him I was coming here but I just couldn't make myself do it."

"I understand. I think," said Zeb, getting to his feet. "Want some time alone now?"

"Just a little while."

He left her. Then in less than two minutes, Emily

tapped on the door and hurried into the room. "I shouldn't have said what I did," she whispered tearfully, touching her daughter's hair. "I'm really sorry, sweetheart."

Squeezing her hand, Leah silently forgave her.

CHAPTER ELEVEN

Jace was miserable. By Wednesday, he'd had enough. Leah hadn't returned his phone call, leaving the next move up to him. He decided to make it. After calling the airport, he showered, dressed, packed a bag, and carried it out to the car. As he swung it into the trunk Buddy strolled out from the barn.

"I was just about to come find you," Jace told his foreman. "I'm going to be gone awhile. Not sure how long."

"Where you taking off to?"

"To see Leah." Jace tossed his tan safari jacket through the open car window onto the front seat. "We need to talk."

"Need to do something, I reckon. Never seen you as touchy as you've been the last couple of days," Buddy said with an understanding nod. "So you're going to go see her at her folks' house. Then what?"

"Like I said, we need to talk."

"Talk's cheap. Action might be better. Why don't you just bring her on back here where she belongs?"

Jace grinned at his friend. "You mean kidnap her?"

"Naw, you won't have to do that."

"Don't be so sure. After all that's happened, she may not want to have anything more to do with me."

"You can sweet-talk her."

"I think I'll have to do more than that." Opening the car door, Jace got into the driver's seat, turned the key in the ignition, and started the engine. "I'd better get going. I have to stop in town before I catch the plane."

"Bring her back with you," Buddy called as the car rolled along the driveway.

"I plan to. Even if I *do* have to kidnap her," Jace answered, waving good-bye.

Jace's flight arrived in Austin at six twelve that evening. He rented a car, and after he'd consulted a road map he drove to Lone Pond. Asking directions from a pedestrian, he easily found the Bancroft place on the other side of the small town. Set off by itself in a grove of oak trees, the cedar shingled house was rustic and appealing. Two cars were parked in the attached garage as he pulled into the driveway. Getting out of the rented Chevy, he pulled on his jacket, went up the flagstone walk to the front door, and rang the bell. When Zeb Bancroft opened the door and saw who was there his face clouded over at once.

Jace felt rather like a specimen being observed under a microscope. He adjusted the open collar of his blue shirt, wondering if he should have worn a suit instead of his casual attire, to make a better impression. But no, if he'd worn a suit, he would have looked like he was *trying* to make a good impression and therefore he wouldn't have. What a ridiculous debate to be having right now. Reassembling his thoughts, he inclined his head at Leah's father.

"Nice to see you again, Mr. Bancroft."

"Jace," the older man warily replied. "This is a surprise."

"I would have called before coming but I thought maybe Leah wouldn't agree to see me if I did. I do need to talk to her."

Zeb beckoned him in and led him to the living room, courteously offering his hospitality. "Have a seat. Leah isn't home right now, but I'll go tell Emily you're here."

When Leah's mother entered the room several moments later, she too looked at Jace with some suspicion. But she smiled faintly as he rose to his feet and remained standing until she was seated on the sofa across from his chair. Zeb joined her, and she glanced at him before turning her full attention back to Jace. "I don't think Leah is expecting you."

"She isn't, but I have to see her." Jace pulled out a cigarette. "Mind if I smoke, Mrs. Bancroft?"

"Not at all."

"Thanks." He lit up, shook out the match, and dropped it into the ashtray on the table next to his chair. "Do you have any idea when Leah will be back?"

"She went to see a movie. It was the five o'clock show, so she should be home soon."

"Do you mind if I wait for her? Unless you have plans for the evening? Don't let me disturb you."

"We don't have any plans."

Zeb Bancroft cleared his throat. "I'm going to be blunt, Jace—that's a right fathers have," he announced, leaning forward on the sofa. "Emily and I didn't know about you and Leah until after you called

Saturday. We'd thought maybe something was bothering her, and so after dinner when I gave her the message we asked a few questions. Now that we know what we do, I have to tell you that I don't want you to stay and wait for her unless you have a damn good reason."

"I do. The best. I love her."

"She doesn't seem at all sure of that."

"Then I'm going to have to convince her," Jace said, leaning forward also, resting his elbows on his knees. "That's what I came to do."

"We want her to be happy."

"I want that too."

"We hope so."

"I do. Trust me."

The couple exchanged glances and visibly relaxed, obviously reassured by his sincere tone. Emily Bancroft served coffee and the conversation became less personal. She and Zeb refrained from asking more questions about his relationship with Leah, and he was clearly grateful for their restraint. An interrogation, hostile or otherwise, was the last thing he needed while waiting for Leah to come in.

About half an hour passed before she did return. The front door opened and Jace heard her voice in the hall, her light laughter mingling with that of a man's. But her laughter abruptly ceased when she came through the door and saw him getting up from his chair.

Astonished at the sight of him, Leah stopped short, her heart jumping and then sinking just as fast. She forced herself to enter the room, all the while frantically wondering why he was there.

"Hi sailor, new in town?" she managed to ask flippantly, giving her parents an unconvincing smile. "That's a joke. Jace was in the navy."

"Yes, dear, you told us that," her mother replied somewhat weakly. Apparently aware of the tension that had suddenly descended over all of them, she tried to ease some of it. "How was the movie? Did you enjoy it?"

"Loved it. It was hilarious, wasn't it, Bill?" Leah turned to the tall lanky young man who had come in with her. He readily agreed, and she introduced him to Jace. "This is my cousin, Bill Warner. Bill, Jace Austin. He owns the ranch across from my house."

The two men greeted each other with a few words and a handshake. Then a dreadful silence filled the room. Feeling as if her throat was closing, Leah had to say something, anything, to break it. She went as nonchalantly as possible to stand before the cold fireplace, and politely inquired, "What brought you here, Jace? In Austin on business?"

"Personal business, yes," he responded, going to her. "I came here specifically to see you. I want to talk to you, Leah."

"All right. Go ahead."

"Alone."

"Uh, I have to run along now," Bill spoke up, rising and going to take Leah's right hand and squeeze it gently. "I'll see you later."

"Zeb, why don't we go for a drive?" Emily added hastily as Bill hurried out. "That will give Leah and Jace a chance to be by themselves."

"You don't have to leave," Jace told them. "Leah and I will go for a drive and talk."

When he moved closer, she tensed. In one way, she ached to throw herself into his arms; in another, she felt she might dissolve in tears if he so much as laid a finger on her. Torn by conflicting emotions, she shook her head, needing at least a semblance of sanctuary. "I'd rather stay here if you don't mind."

"Leah, I'm not going to run your parents out of their own house," he persisted, taking her hand. "Come on."

"But—"

"Let's go. It's a nice night for a drive."

As his long fingers closed around hers, she gave her father a beseeching look that belied the joking tone she attempted. "You're not going to just let him abduct your daughter, are you?"

"He's not abducting you. He only wants to talk," Zeb answered. "I think maybe you should listen to what he has to say."

"But I can listen here as well as anywhere else."

"Don't be stubborn, Leah," Jace murmured, unwilling to indulge in any more verbal fencing. He nodded gratefully to Zeb, and a look of understanding passed between them as he guided her toward the door. "Come with me. Please?"

That one small word defused her explosive desire to resist him long enough for him to escort her outside to his rental car. Waiting until she was settled in the passenger seat, he walked around the car and got in behind the steering wheel. With a flick of his wrist he started the engine. It purred to life, and Leah sat immobile, staring straight ahead, maintaining complete silence as he pulled out of the drive and headed for the general vicinity of Austin.

Only the muted swoosh of the tires skimming over black asphalt permeated the tense quiet between them. Jace glanced sideways at Leah, recognized the obstinate tilt of her small chin, and audibly sighed.

"Your parents are very nice."

"Yes. And obviously, you turned on the old charm for them or Dad wouldn't have let you drag me out of the house like that."

"I didn't drag you out."

"He wouldn't have let you do that Saturday night. After they asked me about you and I told them about us—some of it, anyway—he wasn't very happy with you."

"Maybe now he realizes that he has nothing to worry about."

"How did you manage to con him into believing that?"

Eyes narrowing, Jace ignored that question. "Bill is a nice-looking man," he said.

"Yes, he is. I'll certainly tell him what you said. He'll be glad you think so, I'm sure."

"Is he really your cousin?"

"Well, if he isn't we've been living a lie for years. I was three years old when he was born and the whole family told me he was my new cousin, so I assume he is."

"A simple yes would have been sufficient," Jace muttered, his deep voice grating. "No need for sarcasm."

She glared at him, her green eyes flashing with defiance. "I'll be sarcastic whenever I please, especially when you practically accuse me of lying. Bill's my cousin. Would you like to see his birth certificate and our family tree to see how we're related?"

"I'll take your word for it."

"Aren't you generous. What do you want, Jace? Why did you come all this way to see me?"

"Why did you leave again without bothering to tell me where you were going?" he countered, his voice hard, as he turned into the parking lot of a large park in a suburb two miles outside the Austin city limits. Braking to a stop, he killed the motor. "You should at least have told Buddy where you'd be so he could tell me. You knew I'd be worried."

"I did?" she exclaimed, balling her hands into tight fists in her lap. "The last time we talked, I got the distinct impression you weren't very interested at all in me or anything about me."

"You know better than that. For God's sake, Leah." He reached out for her.

"Don't touch me," she huskily commanded, finding the door handle and scrambling out of the car. She walked across the slope of a well-tended grassy knoll and past the deserted playground to the edge of the sparkling brook that meandered through the park. Jace soon caught up with her and tried to take her arm. She neatly sidestepped him, exclaiming, "What do you want?"

"I want to know if you're coming back."

"To my house?"

"Yes."

What do you think? Don't flatter yourself. Even you can't drive me out of my home. Of course I'm going back."

"When?"

"Sunday."

"Don't wait that long. Fly home with me tomorrow," Jace murmured, moving close behind her to put his arms around her waist and draw her back against him. "I miss you, Leah."

Stiffening, she tried to pull away from him, hurt and resentment welling up inside when he wouldn't release her. "Maybe you just miss having me so conveniently nearby."

"You know it's much more than that."

"I told you last week, I don't know anything about your real feelings. You don't even seem to know how you feel yourself."

"I didn't before, but I do now," he said, his voice soft and low in her ear. "I need you with me. I love you."

"You've said that before. How long will you love me this time, Jace? Until tomorrow? The next day? Next week?" She turned her head, trying to escape the fluttering caress of his breath. "I won't let you use me, Jace."

"I've never used you."

"Damn you," she exploded, struggling to get free, tormented by his touch and raw emotion. "You did use me, by wanting nothing more than to spend the night with me once in a while."

"I understand that that's the way it must seem."

"It doesn't just seem that way, it is that way. The way you made it, all because of the lousy experience you had with Erica."

"I wasn't sure about us, I admit it," he said, turning her around to face him, his hands curving around her upper arms. In the orange glow of the setting sun, he looked into her eyes. "But a man can change his mind and I've changed mine. I want every night with you from now on. Since you've been gone, I've felt empty without you."

"Jace," she whispered, searching his tanned face for some sign of duplicity. She found none. It was obvious he meant what he was saying now, but would he still be able to say it and mean it later? Anguish mantled her features as she gazed up at him. "I wish I could believe you."

"Leah, you can. I'm talking about making a real commitment."

Hope flowered in her, and she had to fight to restrain it. "What kind of commitment do you mean?"

"How about forever?" he asked softly, tipping her chin up with one finger. "I want us to be together for the rest of our lives." He gave her a wry smile. "I never imagined I could say that to anyone, so soon after Erica. But you're something special, lady."

"What if you stop thinking so? What if you start remembering the awful times with Erica again?"

"I can't let the mistake I made by marrying her control me the rest of my life. When the marriage ended, I decided to wait a few years before getting involved with anyone again, but you upset that plan. There you were, right across the road, and I fell in love. It seemed too soon so I tried to fight it."

"But Jace, you—"

He kissed her briefly. "I'm not going to risk losing you again, Leah."

"But I—"

Kissing her again, he allowed his lips to linger upon hers a moment. "You are special. And mine."

"I'd be crazy to—"

Once more he kissed her, longer this time. "If you don't promise to go home with me tomorrow, I really will kidnap you and take you back tonight. I think I could probably even get your father's permission, since I convinced him and your mother you mean everything to me."

"I must be crazy," she murmured, needing him as always, and feeling herself slowly surrender to that need.

His mouth came down firmly on hers, parting her lips.

"I am crazy," she moaned, her slender fingers tightly clutching his shirtfront as she kissed him back. "You're taking advantage of my feelings for you."

"A man does what he has to."

"And I'm letting you do it. I shouldn't."

"But you want to."

"Yes. And I may live to regret it. If you do change your mind about us again, I—"

"You're a hard woman to convince. I thought you might be. That's why I brought this along." Stepping back, his smile indulgent, he removed a velvet jeweler's box from the pocket of his jacket, opened it, and showed her the ring inside. "Believe I'm serious now?"

Tears filled her eyes, blurring the oval diamond set in platinum and gold. He slipped it onto her finger. Stunned by the unexpected gesture, she shook her head incredulously. "An engagement ring?"

"Diamonds usually mean a man and woman are engaged," was his wry answer. "I understand marriage is coming back in style. That is what you want, isn't it?"

"Yes," she confessed, unable to lie even for the

sake of pride. "But is it what *you* want?"

"Would you like me to go down on one knee and make a formal proposal?"

"No, don't," she said, stopping him as he started to do just that. Uncertainty darkened her eyes as they held his. "I'm being very serious, Jace. I don't want us to get married if you feel forced into it."

"You know me better than that. Nobody can force me to do anything."

"But—"

"Leah, don't you start causing us problems. I did enough of that for both of us," he said, taking her in his arms. "I want us to get married as soon as possible. All you have do is say yes. Will you?"

"Oh Jace, yes. Yes," she throatily murmured, persuaded at last. Her kiss met his as she wound her arms around his neck, and he hugged her so hard that he lifted her off the ground. Sheer joy made her giddy. Holding him, being held, was heavenly, and she offered a heartfelt silent prayer of thanks that she hadn't lost him after all. It was so good to be with him again, even better than ever now that she was sure of his love.

"I'm so happy," she whispered against his neck. "Thank you for the ring, Jace. I adore it. It's beautiful."

"You're beautiful," he whispered back, taking swift possession of her lips once more.

In the quiet of the empty park, by the babbling brook, they shared kiss after kiss, each lengthening and becoming more intense. Jace's hands cupped the straining sides of Leah's breasts, and trembling, she took his hand to lead him beneath the low-hanging bough of a willow tree that provided a perfect hideaway.

She undid her belt. "Let's make love."

"Here?"

She laughed at his surprised expression. "Yes, here. We certainly can't go back to my folks' house and ask them to excuse us while we go to my bedroom. Dad might believe you care about me, but believe me, he'd draw the line at that."

"We could go to a motel."

"I can't wait that long. I need you now," she said, pulling her denim jumper over her head. She wore only a bra and panties beneath it. After ridding Jace of his jacket and shirt, she stepped her fingertips up and down his powerful arms. "Besides, we've never made love outdoors before, and this is the perfect place, secluded and pretty. Come on, Jace, make me feel like a wood nymph."

"Naughty wench," he replied, unhooking her bra and freeing her breasts to his hands and mouth. "You can be such a provocative vixen. That's one of the reasons I love you so much."

"How much, Jace?" she breathed. "Show me."

He stripped her and then undressed himself. His hands coursed over her as a light breeze whispered through the narrow leaves that formed a pale green curtain around them.

He lowered her to the soft springy grass, doing wonderful things to her as she caressed him, her parted lips clinging sweetly to his. Whispering endearments, they joined together, creating an inseparable bond of love and passion. He adored her with his eyes, his hands, all of him, and she felt as much a part of him as he was of her.

"I do love you. More than I can say," he said roughly, watching the soft light in her eyes, transfixed by the warmth they conveyed. "I'll never let you go now. You know that, don't you?"

"You'll never be able to get rid of me, because I love you too. More than anything." She ran her fingers through the thick hair that brushed his neck. "I'm going to stay with you forever."

"Longer than that," he declared, cradling the back of her head in one hand as he kissed her again ... and again.

In their hideaway, they loved as they never had. He was free of the past and she was free of the fear of heartache. Twilight stole in around them, darkening the shadows in their private bower while they found ecstasy together. They knew each other so well, understood each other's hopes and dreams and thoughts. And this time it was better than it had ever been, because the words of love they freely exchanged made all the difference. When they soared up to the throbbing heights of completion it was all the more exquisite, as they took in full measure as much as they gave, sharing every glorious second.

Later, lying in the crook of Jace's arm, Leah lifted her left hand to admire the shining diamond ring. "It's lovely. I like it so much and it's a perfect fit. How did you know what size to get?"

"I went over to your house and borrowed your pearl ring to take to the jeweler."

"You are a sneaky man."

"Mmm, when I have to be. I went to your house to find your folks' address too."

"I'm so glad you did."

"So am I," he said, playing with a wisp of her golden hair. "Leah, I didn't know lovemaking could mean this much."

"I didn't either, really. I hoped it could."

He chuckled softly. "Some women are such romantics. You're one of them."

"Hey neighbor," she retaliated, "you better watch those sexist remarks."

"I'm not your neighbor anymore. Even if we wait a few days or a week to get married, I want you to move over to the ranch with me. And I won't take no for an answer."

"I wouldn't dream of saying no."

"Your house? Do you think you'll want to sell it?"

"I'd rather rent it. I don't want to let it go completely."

"Because you put so much work into it?"

"That, and because moving there brought me to you."

"See? I told you you're a romantic," he teased. "You know, it just occurred to me. I'll be getting a nice little fringe benefit by marrying you. A photographer in the family. Think how much money we'll save on pictures of the children."

She poked him in the ribs. "What a time to talk about saving money. And listen to you. You mentioned children. When I did that quite innocently, I remind you—you almost headed for the hills."

Low laughter rumbled up in him. "I did, didn't I? Well, everything's different now. I do want us to have children. But let's wait awhile. I'm going to want you all to myself for a long time."

"Sounds good to me." She kissed him, dancing her lips playfully over his. "Would you really have kidnapped me if I hadn't given in to your charm?"

"What do you think?"

"I think you might have. At your barbecue Hattie Briscoe told me you were more than willing to go after whatever you wanted."

"Hattie's right. And tonight, I wanted you. I always will, Leah," he promised, sitting up, pulling her up beside him. "I think it's time to go tell your folks we're making wedding plans, don't you?"

In the waning light they helped each other dress. Then they walked across the empty playground and through the quiet park to the car, holding hands. In the soft glow of a streetlight, Jace halted, turned her to face him, and kissed her repeatedly. "I love you. Always remember that."

"And I love you. You told me what a great marriage your parents had, Jace," she said earnestly, lacing her fingers through his. "If I can't guarantee ours will be as wonderful, I think there's a good chance it could be."

"I think so, too, because we're both willing to work hard at making it wonderful."

"And I'm more than willing to try my best," she told him. Then she grinned. "There is one condition, though. Before the wedding, you have to promise I can keep my chickens."

He laughed. "Honey, you could probably convince me to turn the whole ranch into a chicken farm."

"I doubt that."

"Don't underestimate your power. A man hopelessly in love can be very susceptible. And very happy," he added, pulling her into his arms and burying his face in her silken hair. She was the right woman for him. Deep in his heart, he knew that without a doubt.

She hugged him hard, then gazed up into his loving blue eyes. In their depths, she found a home warmer and more fulfilling than she had ever known, and her own eyes offered the same to him.

A gentle smile curved his lips. It was an offer he accepted. Life was suddenly even more precious.

He kissed her again.

ROMANTIC TIMES MAGAZINE
the magazine for romance novels ...and the women who read them!

♥ **EACH MONTHLY ISSUE** features over 120 Reviews & Ratings, saving you time and money when browsing at the bookstores!

ALSO INCLUDES...
♥ A Fun Readers Section
♥ Author Profiles
♥ Industry News & Gossip

PLUS...

♥ Interviews with the **Hottest Hunk Cover Models** in romance such as: Fabio, Steve Sandalis, John D'Salvo & many more!

♥ **Order a SAMPLE COPY Now!** ♥

COST: $2.00 (includes postage & handling)

CALL 1-800-989-8816*
*800 Number for credit card orders only
Visa • MC • AMEX • Discover Accepted!

♥ **BY MAIL:** Make check payable to:
Romantic Times Magazine, 55 Bergen Street, Brooklyn, NY 11201
♥ **PHONE:** 718-237-1097   ♥ **FAX:** 718-624-4231
♥ **E-MAIL:** RTmag1@aol.com ♥ **WEBSITE:** http://www.rt-online.com

Also Available in Bookstores and on Newsstands!

About the Author

Donna Kimel Vitek is a true pioneer among romance writers, having written over 30 novels since the '70s. She now lives in Winston Salem, North Carolina.